BREATH OF LIFE
(A GAIAN CONSORTIUM NOVELLA)

CHRISTINE POPE

DARK VALENTINE PRESS

Breath of Life

This is a work of fiction. Names, characters, places, and incidents are either the product of the author's imagination or are used fictitiously. Any resemblance to actual events, places, organizations, or persons, whether living or dead, is entirely coincidental.

BREATH OF LIFE

ISBN: 978-0615654812

Published by Dark Valentine Press

Cover and interior design by Indie Author Services

Please visit www.christinepope.com to learn more about this author.

For everyone who loved the original story…

BREATH OF LIFE

Lathvin IV, Gaian Relocation Corporation Colony 223

MY FAMILY PROBABLY WASN'T THE FIRST to be deceived by the Gaia Relocation Corporation's advertising materials, and I know they won't be the last. However, that's little consolation when you're stuck on a rock light-years from where you were born, scrabbling to make enough to keep your homestead going and maybe put enough aside so that you'll get something a little fancier than a plain plastic box when it's time for you to depart this mortal coil.

Homesteading on Lathvin IV sounded great on paper, I guess. At least, my parents went for it as a way of escaping our subterranean existence on Gaia's moon, and my older sister Libba and I couldn't do much except just go along for the ride. She was the lucky one, anyway—she's two years older than I, and got a full scholarship to the university at Epsilon Eridani, and so she bailed out at the first opportunity. By then we were all heartily sick of the constant need for breathing equipment every time we wanted to go outside, and the faint chugging sound of the atmospheric generator, which filtered through all our waking hours and our sleeping ones as well. I used to have nightmares about being trapped in the bowels of some enormous ship where all I could hear was that low-level *boom boom boom.* Sure, you couldn't walk around outside on the moon without a full suit, but you didn't need to anyway, as pretty much all of the moon's infrastructure was located beneath the surface. There, you could just leave your apartment and walk down a hallway to catch the subway or go shopping or to school or what-have-you. Not so on Lathvin, where our nearest neighbors on one side were an unfriendly older couple whose homestead was a good five kilometers off, and on the other…

One minor detail the Gaia Relocation Corporation neglected to make clear was Lathvin's status as a Gaian-only homestead. Turns out the claim had been disputed by the Zhore, who said they'd discovered the world first and therefore had the only true settlement rights. That hadn't stopped the GRC from dumping a whole bunch of unsuspecting colonists on the planet about ten years prior to the time my family got there. The whole mess had ended up in the sector's High Court, which ruled that we had to play nice and share, because there weren't a whole heck of a lot of worlds out there in the habitable range.

So, the Zhore. No one knew what they looked like. Whenever they went out in public, they were invariably cloaked in heavy black robes and hoods that concealed every inch of their bodies, along with breathing masks that covered their entire faces (which wasn't really necessary; the standard breather most people used just went over your nose and mouth). About all anyone knew was the Zhore tended to be the same basic size and shape as humans, although they skewed a little taller, and they breathed approximately the same type of atmosphere humans did, as the mix coming out of their atmospheric generators didn't differ materially from what spewed from ours. But that was about it, even though I did as much searching on the subject in the planetary database as my security levels would allow. Since I, Anika Jespers, was a colonist's daughter with absolutely zero security clearances, that wasn't much.

Anyway, our next closest neighbor was a Zhore, even though we'd never seen him. It. Whatever. No one seemed to be terribly clear on gender and the Zhore, either. However, since I didn't really like thinking of a fellow sentient being as "it," I always thought of our neighbor as a he, even though I suppose he could have been a she. Or even an it, I guessed, if I put my own feelings on the nomenclature aside. A few alien species were gender-neutral, after all.

The Zhore's homestead was much larger than ours, both in acreage and the size of the house that had been erected on it. We watched it being built, as the alien had arrived on the scene after we'd been living on Lathvin for about six years. The house was a massive, vaguely threatening pile, made of native dark-gray Lathvin stone. It must have cost a fortune. At least, that's what my father always said. It had two atmospheric generators and an enormous clear polymer-covered structure around back that he thought might be a greenhouse. All around the Zhore's house grew fields and fields of moonflowers.

No, that's not their scientific name, but all the colonists called them that. Native flowers with pale heads wide as a dinner plate, and with the peculiar ability to give off large amounts of oxygen, even after they'd been cut. I asked once why we didn't just grow moonflowers instead of using the generators, and was told that, while they produced enough O_2 to keep you from asphyxiating in Lathvin IV's thin air, there was no way they'd ever make enough to cover the planet in a breathable atmosphere. Okay, fine.

They were pretty, though.

Storms came and went on Lathvin all the time. We were used to them, used to their violence. The engineers always said that was to be expected, that during the atmosphere-building stages wind currents and weather patterns were unusually volatile. But one day, when my father had gone into Port Natchez to pick up supplies, the winds kept increasing in intensity, buffeting our little prefab house and screaming through every chink and crevice. I turned up the heat on our climate-control unit and tried not to think about my father making his way home in that maelstrom. After all, the transport, while not exactly new and shiny, did have geo-locators and all-terrain treads, and would no doubt soldier through this storm just as it had hundreds before.

My mother stayed home that day as well; I'd begun to notice a disconcerting tendency in her to do almost anything she could to avoid going outside. True, Lathvin could be pretty oppressive. Clouds given birth by the atmospheric generators roiled overhead almost around the clock, and it rained a good deal. If you saw the sun twice a year, you were lucky. Most of the time it didn't bother me too much, as we didn't exactly engage in a lot of outdoor activity when we lived on the moon, either. True, when my sister Libba would send us a vidmail where she looked conspicuously bronzed, and then waxed a little too rhapsodic about sitting in outdoor cafes on Epsilon Eridani or swimming in an actual ocean, of all things—well, then, of course I'd feel little green spikes of jealousy. Who wouldn't? Otherwise, though, I tried to see some beauty in the shapes of the bruise-colored clouds that swirled across the sky, or in the pale faces of the moonflowers and the odd, blood-colored ground cover that was the only other thing that seemed to grow on Lathvin. Some days I was more successful than others.

The minutes and then hours ticked by with no word from my father, and at last I didn't bother to make even a pretense of studying. I logged off from the university's site and turned away from my workstation. My mother had a tablet computer in her lap and wireless buds firmly lodged in her ears; I guessed she wasn't paying any attention to me. She could have been working, or maybe not. It was hard to tell with her sometimes. She was connected to that tablet more often than not, and I sometimes wondered if she used the excuse of having to push little electronic bits of data around so she wouldn't have to deal with her family.

"It's nineteen hundred," I said.

She didn't blink.

I got up from my chair, crossed the room, and stood directly in front of her. "It's nineteen hundred," I said again, this time a little more loudly. All right, a lot more loudly.

Then she did lift her head, although her dark eyes still looked unfocused. "What?"

"Dad should have been home two hours ago."

"Oh?" she said vaguely, and glanced around the shabby chamber that served as our combination living/dining room. "Well, he's been late before. Are you hungry?"

"No, I'm not hungry," I replied, and tried to quell the little flare of exasperation that rose inside me. "I'm worried about Dad. This storm is brutal."

She shrugged. I didn't know whether the shrug meant she was indifferent to his fate, or simply that she knew the situation wasn't worth getting worked up over. My parents didn't fight—at least, not so I ever heard them, no mean feat in a house as small as ours. But I'd sensed an underlying unease that had been building for years. Resentment over coming to Lathvin IV. Bitterness over being stuck here with no chance of escape. It wasn't as simple as just walking out, either. Married couples had to sign a joint contract, or they wouldn't get the homestead. If she left Dad and tried to go back to Gaia's moon, he'd lose the house and everything they'd been working toward for the past ten years.

Even though I knew all that, something about the negligent little shrug made me want to slap her. My own mother. I gritted my teeth and forced myself to walk away and look out the window. I was just tired. All this online studying, and for what? So I'd have a certificate to show people, so I could get a job shoving bytes around the way my mother did? They acted like my schooling was important, but I knew better. The only one of us who had any chance at all was Libba.

The view outside the window didn't do much to improve my mood. Rain came down in heavy curtains, and the only reason I could see even that much was because of the security lights we had installed along the outer perimeter of the property. I told myself that my father had driven the route between Port Natchez and the homestead a thousand times, that he could probably do it blindfolded if necessary. Or maybe he was late because the storm had hit while he was still in town, and he'd decided to ride it out there in the Filling Station, the local pub, or maybe in the commissary. No point in waiting for a call, as the storms made civilian communications more than erratic. Oftentimes it was easier to just head where you were going rather than wait to get a clear signal.

After a while I turned away from the window. I knew I couldn't stand there all night, so I went into the kitchen and pretended to be useful by making a pot of tea and power-defrosting some soup I'd put together a few days earlier. Some time during the past several years I'd taken over most of the cooking, and somehow I hadn't even noticed. At least it gave me something to do.

Neither of us ate much. I cleared away the dishes but left a bowl of soup to warm in the kitchen's heating unit. Maybe I was using that bowl of soup as a shield against uncertainty—after all, how could anything be wrong with my father when he had hot soup waiting for him back home? Stupid, but I didn't know what else to do.

I went back to the computer, not because I thought I'd retain one single fact, but simply because I had to pretend I was doing something. My mother reinserted her ear buds and started typing away on her tablet.

Another hour crawled by, and then another. I knew exactly how much time passed because I kept staring at the little clock in the lower corner of the computer screen. At the moment it seemed far more important than xenolinguistics.

The front door banged open. My father stumbled inside, rain cascading off his all-weather poncho and pooling onto the floor. At once I jumped up from the computer station and ran to him. My mother took out one ear bud and sent a halfway inquiring glance in his direction.

As I reached up to help him with the water-soaked poncho, I noticed how he was shaking, his face almost white above the dark gray polymer-impregnated fabric.

And for some reason he wouldn't look at me, even as I undid the snaps and tossed the poncho into a corner. At least I didn't have to worry about all the water hurting the close-pile carpet underfoot; it was designed to soak up moisture and was pretty much impervious to dirt.

"Dad?" I said. "Are you okay?"

He still wouldn't look at me, but crossed the room and fell rather than sat down on the beat-up sofa my parents been talking about replacing for years. Once there, he hunched over, his hands clasped between his knees.

"Peter?" my mother asked. She sounded almost concerned.

Then he did look up. Whatever had happened on the trip home, it had taken its toll — shadows smudged the skin below his eyes, and every line on his face seemed somehow deeper than it had been before he left. Finally his gaze fastened on me. His lips compressed, and then he said, "Anika, I've done something terrible."

"What?" I couldn't imagine my father, who sometimes could be misguided but who I knew was incapable of hurting anyone, doing something so wrong that it had aged him ten years in a single day.

He looked past me to my mother. "The transport is wrecked. Ran off the road about seven kilometers from here. I thought I could walk home."

She bit her lip. We all knew that even with insurance replacing the transport would be difficult. We'd been nursing the vehicle along for years. Transports newly drop-shipped here cost far more than what our meager insurance would give us for the wrecked vehicle.

I said reassuringly, "It's okay, Dad. The important thing is that you're home safe and you're all right."

The glance he gave me was so wretched, so full of despair, that I couldn't help taking a step back.

"Is it?" He shook his head. "Sit down, Anika. I have something I need to tell you."

Since I didn't know what else to do, I did sit down, even though my stomach knotted and little shivers of dread began crawling down the back of my neck. Whatever he had to say, it couldn't be good.

Without really looking at either my mother or me, he went on, "I'd never seen rain like this before, but I knew the road...or I thought I did. It's washed out—I went over the side and hit a boulder. Still, I had my breathing equipment, and I knew about where I was. It wouldn't be a pleasant walk, but I didn't want to wait on the off chance that a patrol might come by. So I grabbed what I could and left."

I said nothing, but only watched as his hands twisted around themselves, almost as if they'd taken on a life of their own and he was powerless to stop them.

"I walked for a long while," he went on. "Then my breath got short, and I stopped to look at the gauge on my breather. It was fine—it had to be fine, as I'd double-checked it right before I left town. But it wasn't." He lifted his shoulders, even as he frowned. "The membrane must've gotten torn in the crash or something. I knew I was still at least four kilometers from home, and there was no way I'd make it with what I had left." He hesitated. "I kept going. What else was I supposed to do? And then I saw them, off to my right."

"Saw what, Dad?"

His hands finally ceased their wringing and instead hung limply over his knees. "Moonflowers. Fields of them. I knew the only way I could survive would be to take as many of them with me as I could. So I went into the nearest field and began cutting them down with my utility knife. Had about a half-dozen gathered when I heard…" He shook his head. "I can't describe it. A shout, or a cry, or maybe a combination of the two. And I looked up to see a Zhore bearing down on me."

"A—Zhore?" I asked. Then my brain caught up with the situation. "You mean our neighbor?"

"If you can even call him that." My father stared down at his hands as if he'd never seen them before. "I apologized for trespassing—told him my breather had malfunctioned and that I needed the flowers or I would die. He told me he didn't care to hear my excuses, that I had been stealing his property."

"You really spoke to him?" I asked. Despite the dire expression on my father's face, I couldn't help being just a little excited. After all, so few people had ever exchanged even that many words with one of the elusive aliens. "What did he sound like?"

"What did he—" A shake of the head, followed by, "He sounded like a man, I suppose. An angry man. I told him that

I was no thief, and offered to pay for the flowers. He didn't say anything to me for a few seconds. Finally he replied, 'I have no use for your money. What else do you have to offer?'

"I told him I was only a homesteader, that all I had was my little bit of land and my family. That seemed to interest him, and he asked who my family members were. So I told him about my wife, and my daughter in college off-world…and I told him of you, Anika."

I didn't see how that had any bearing on the situation, but I decided not to say anything. I worried that any more interruptions might stop my father from telling the rest of his story.

"The Zhore made a sound that might have been a laugh," my father went on, his words coming more and more slowly, as if he had to drag them out of himself. "And he said—he said—" He broke off, and knotted his hands in his wet hair. For the first time I realized just how gray that hair had gotten over the past ten years.

"Said what, Peter?" my mother inquired, as she took out the second ear bud and laid her tablet aside. Maybe she really did care about what he had to say after all.

"He said he would forgive me my theft if I—" My father licked his pale lips and said, "If I brought my daughter to him."

A heavy silence fell, as my mother and I exchanged puzzled glances. What use could a Zhore have with a human girl? Never mind the fact that what our alien neighbor had proposed was even more illegal than the minor trespassing and petty theft he'd accused my father of. There were some sectors of the galaxy where people were traded like commodities—or so I'd read, anyway—but Lathvin IV wasn't located in one of them.

"A horrible joke?" I asked, and my father shook his head.

"No, Anika. I tried to tell him what he asked was impossible—and illegal—but he wouldn't listen. Told me to breathe of the flowers, as by then my own oxygen supply had almost run out, and I did. I wanted to have enough breath to argue with him, if nothing else. He said he could make things difficult for me—bring me up against the magistrate. He pointed out that if the ruling went against me, I could lose the homestead."

"Well, we can't let that happen," I said, my tone flat. Crazy as it might have seemed to someone outside the situation, somehow complaining about giving myself over as chattel to a vindictive alien seemed petty when measured against the possibility of losing the piece of land we'd struggled to survive on all those years.

My father replied, "It's insane, and we all know it. We can fight this thing—"

"With what?" my mother interjected. "We don't have money for a lawyer. Are you going to defend yourself? We've all seen this Zhore's property—he can probably afford to hire an army of lawyers if he needs to."

I knew she was right, but somehow it didn't feel that great to listen to my mother calmly point out all the reasons why it would make much more sense for me to hand myself over like a good girl. Technically, at twenty I was considered an adult and could do as I wished, but the truth was that I depended on them for everything. The best way I could help them now was to go to the Zhore.

"It's all right, Dad," I said, my voice calm enough, even though an odd, fluttery sensation had started somewhere in my midsection. "We all know there's no way you can let him take you to court. You've worked so hard on this homestead—I won't let you lose it."

His eyes looked suspiciously bright, but he stared back at me without flinching. "And I won't let my daughter give herself over to a monster."

"I've been of age for almost three years. You really can't stop me." The words sounded firm and reasonable. I almost believed them.

A few seconds passed, seconds in which he sat there and watched me as if he hadn't really ever seen me before. "You mean that?"

"Yes," I said. "You've done so much for me. Let me do something now to help you."

He was silent, but somehow in the sudden slump of his shoulders I saw he wouldn't fight me anymore.

"Besides," I added, and managed to summon a smile, "I'm ready for a change."

I had spoken only to hearten my father, to attempt to erase the miserable look on his face, but I realized once I had said the words that I actually did mean them.

Only after I packed my few meager belongings did I understand how little I had accumulated during our years here on Lathvin IV. Some changes of clothing, the precious gold ring my parents had given me for my eighteenth birthday and which I knew they really couldn't afford. My own tablet computer, smaller than my mother's and not as powerful. I used the desk computer for my schoolwork, as the tablets weren't set up to connect to the subspace grid, but of course I couldn't exactly take that with me. Somehow I doubted the Zhore would allow me to continue my studies, but if he did, well, he was rich enough to get me my own desktop unit with subspace relays.

The storm had blown itself out, but the world was still sodden as my father and I set forth. My mother begged off, saying her head ached. I wanted to hate her for her cowardice, but maybe it was easier for her to make her farewells inside the familiar walls of her own home. An odd numbness had overtaken me, and I could only hug her briefly before I followed my father out to the airlock.

The Zhore's instructions had been that I should come immediately, even though by that time it was almost twenty-three hundred. They used Gaia time on Lathvin, even though the planet's natural day only had twenty-two hours; our hours were shorter than Gaia standard to compensate. Still, late was late, no matter how you calculated it.

I wore my breather and my father had the spare. They were designed so you could communicate easily when wearing them, but neither of us seemed too inclined to conversation. My father carried a halogen torch, and I my little satchel with all my worldly goods. I concentrated on the treacherous ground underfoot; of course the road was well-paved, but mud had flowed across sections of it. In a few days someone would come along with a 'dozer to clear it out, I supposed. In the meantime, we picked our way along and tried not to trip over scattered rocks or stumble into a hole.

Despite the rough going, we reached the perimeter of the Zhore's property sooner than I would have liked. The moonflowers danced and swayed around us, seeming to laugh in the darkness. A dark path wound through them toward the Zhore's house.

We stopped there. My father said, "You can't do this, Anika."

Somehow I'd known he would make one last attempt to keep me from going. I shook my head, wishing that so much of our faces weren't obscured by the breathing apparatus. There were newer, more streamlined models available, but purchasing them had been beyond our modest means. "It'll be fine. It's really like I'm hardly leaving at all. Libba's the one who's light-years and light-years away—I'll just be a few kilometers down the road."

His cheeks moved, and I guessed he smiled a little behind the breathing mask. "I see I really can't stop you."

"No," I said. "Let me do this, Dad. Let me help."

And then he took me and gave me a fierce hug before he turned away, as if he couldn't bear to watch me walk up the path to the Zhore's house. It was all right. I didn't think I'd want to do that, either, if our roles had been reversed.

So there was no one to see me move down the dark path through all those pale flowers, which sighed and rustled in the dark. I kept my head up and walked steadily toward the looming bulk of the Zhore's home—mansion, really, now that I grew closer and saw how big the place actually was. It looked like pictures I'd seen of old houses on Gaia, except something seemed slightly off about the proportions, and the windows had odd little arches above them. Two lights burned blue-white at the entrance, one on either side of an enormous pewter-colored door. As I approached, the door swung inward, opening on an air-lock much grander than the one at our homestead. This one looked almost like a vestibule of its own.

Maybe the Zhore had been watching on a closed cir-cuit, or maybe the door was programmed to open when-ever someone came near it. I supposed it really didn't matter. I had set myself on this course, and so I'd have to follow through, no matter what happened.

I stepped inside, then waited for the familiar *whoosh* of the door sealing behind me. I reached up and took off the breathing mask. Fresh air, with none of the faintly recycled scent of the air of my family's homestead, swirled around me.

The interior door opened then, and I stepped out into an enormous room fully two stories high, with a wide stair-case directly in front of me. Lights in sconces burned at half-power, gleaming off floors and walls of what appeared to be dark, polished stone. In one corner a wall fountain splashed into the silence.

"Welcome." The voice was deep and calm, and seemed to come from a spot halfway up the stairs.

I started, then realized what I thought had been just another shadow was the Zhore himself, standing there in his night-colored robes. Of course, I could see nothing of him, just the vague outline of a hooded figure. He did seem very tall.

"Thank you," I said. What a silly thing to say. Why should I be thanking him for blackmailing me away from my family and my home? I added, in a slightly sharper tone, "That is, I'm here because you didn't give us much choice."

To my surprise, he laughed. The laugh sounded human enough at least, although I knew no human being lurked beneath those concealing robes. "You are not afraid to speak your mind. That is good." A pause, then, "Come here."

I wanted to refuse, but I doubted that would do me or my cause much good. Clutching my satchel, I mounted the basalt staircase and stopped on the step just below him. He surveyed me for a moment.

"What is your name?"

"Anika," I replied. "Anika Jespers."

"Anika," he repeated. "What does it mean?"

"Mean?"

"All names have meanings, don't they?"

I supposed that was mostly true, but I found myself reluctant to give him an answer. "My parents said it meant 'beautiful' in one of the old Gaian languages." I shrugged. "Sorry about the false advertising."

"You are not considered beautiful?"

How was I supposed to reply to that? Libba had always been considered the golden child, with her strawberry blonde hair and big green eyes. If a person had been feeling charitable, they might have referred to my hair as dark auburn in certain lights, but really, it was plain reddish-brown, and while I was pretty enough according to Gaian standards, I didn't think anyone except an indulgent parent would have ever thought of me as beautiful.

"Not by people who've had their eyes recently checked," I said.

Another laugh. "Zhore eyes are sharper than human eyes," he commented, rather cryptically. "Come—I will show you to your room."

Failing any other alternatives, I followed him upstairs, where he led me down a long hall to a doorway with a palm lock.

"Put your hand on it, so it can learn your print," he instructed me, and I pulled off my glove and set my palm against the cool glass surface. A second or two passed, and then a blue light came on, and the door slid open.

I hadn't really known quite what to expect—maybe that he'd put me to work in the kitchen or tending the plants hidden in the greenhouse at the back of his property—but what I hadn't expected was a room almost as big as my parents' entire house, with sleek furniture of some pale polished material I couldn't identify, and a bed covered in silky fabric in an elusive aquamarine shade.

"It's beautiful," I said in awed tones, before I thought that maybe I shouldn't seem quite so grateful. After all, I was here under duress. The most luxurious bedroom in the galaxy couldn't change that.

The hooded head tilted slightly. "I am glad it pleases you. The closet is there, behind that door, and the door opposite goes to the washroom. You will want to sleep, I should think. It is quite late."

That much was true. Still, something made me blurt out, "But…why am I here? Those threats to my father, just so you could have a house guest?"

Silence for a few seconds, and then he said only, "You are tired. We will speak tomorrow."

He turned and left. The door hissed shut behind him. It was only after I stood there for a minute, staring at the swirl-polished metal, that I realized I had never asked him his name.

I overslept, despite the strange bed. Or maybe because of it—my bed at home was lumpy and thin, while the bed the Zhore had given me was made of some soft material that seemed to cushion and cradle every inch of my body. The washroom provided similar luxury, with a polished granite shower and unlimited hot water—at least, it seemed unlimited, as I stood under the warm, pulsing spray for at least a quarter-hour with no sign of it letting up or the familiar warning buzzer telling me I was hitting the danger zone. Back home we'd always had to ration the water so we didn't go over our allotment and get charged extra.

It seemed a shame to have to climb into my plain old gray coveralls after all that decadence, but there wasn't much need for high fashion on a homestead, even if we could have afforded to buy fancier clothes. Once I was done getting dressed I halfway thought the door wouldn't open for me, that I'd been locked in, but it slipped aside without any fuss and allowed me to enter the hallway unchecked.

The house was as gloomy and magnificent as it had been the night before. Lathvin IV's days were about as somber as its nights, and so the Zhore's house was still illuminated by the same artificial lighting I'd seen when I first arrived. I had no idea whether a Zhore home would follow the same layout as a human one, but it seemed logical that the kitchen and therefore the dining room or other eating chamber would be located on the ground floor.

Rain beat against the windows; it appeared I'd been granted enough grace to walk here last night without getting soaked, but that was as far as the weather seemed ready to cooperate. I realized then, as I stood on the bottom step of the huge staircase, that I had no idea what kind of schedule the Zhore might follow. It was entirely possible his race was a nocturnal one and that he'd greeted me last night just as he was getting ready to start his day. True, he had said it was very late. That might have just been a recognition of my human clock, though.

But then I heard him say, "Good morning, Anika," and I turned to see him waiting in a doorway off to the right that led to a room I hadn't yet seen.

"Good morning," I said. I went on, "I never asked you your name last night. It was rude, I suppose."

"You were tired," he replied.

Still I could see nothing of his face, as his hood was constructed to droop so low that it covered him all the way down to his chin. If he had a chin, of course.

He added, "It was understandable. You may call me Sarzhin."

"All right…Sarzhin." It felt odd to address him so plainly, but at least he didn't want me calling him "lord and master" or some other nonsense. As my father had said, the Zhore's voice did sound quite human, even if it was deeper than my father's voice or the voices of the men I knew in Port Natchez. For some reason, that only discomfited me further. Shouldn't an alien have sounded… alien?

"You are hungry?" he asked.

I nodded, even though I couldn't repress the flutter of apprehension that moved through my midsection. Who knows what kind of food the Zhore ate? Maybe I'd get to see his face if we ate together. Of course, that might not be such a good thing. Rumors swirled about the Zhore, and how they must be hideous because they wouldn't let anyone see what they looked like, but that was just human speculation. No one really knew anything.

"Then come in," he told me, and moved out of the way so I could enter the room after him.

It was definitely the dining room, or at least what I'd learned from vids and books that a dining room should look like. We'd never had the space for a chamber like this, either on the homestead or back in our apartment on the moon. My family ate shoulder to shoulder at a round table that might have comfortably fit two. This place, though — I counted twelve chairs around the shining black table's length, though only two places at the far end were set, with gleaming metal plates and glasses in a deep shade of cobalt.

So he did plan to eat. Another of those nervous little tremors passed through me, but I went and took a seat anyway, at the place setting to the right of the table's head. I wasn't about to presume to sit there. He went past me to pull out the chair reserved for the master of the house, so I supposed I had done the right thing. It was sort of difficult to know the etiquette involved in these situations when I'd spent my whole life sitting at a round table.

I wondered whether he had Zhore servants, or maybe humans for whom homesteading hadn't worked out. There were quite a few of those in Port Natchez; they worked in the pub or the commissary or over at the spaceport, and a lot of them weren't above taking on the occasional odd job if one came along. Steady work in a rich Zhore's household might not be such a bad gig.

But then I heard a soft whirring noise, and a gleaming humanoid shape drifted into the dining room, carrying a tray filled with food. My eyes widened a bit. Oh, I'd seen a few mechanoids from time to time at the spaceport, whenever a contingent from the GRC or possibly the Atmospheric Development Agency came by, but no one I personally knew could afford one. Despite all the human race's technological advances, biological muscle was still cheaper than mechanical.

Obviously the Zhore — Sarzhin, I reminded myself — didn't suffer such financial constraints. I tried not to stare as the mechanoid set a plate in front of me and then placed one in front of its master.

"Thank you," Sarzhin said.

The mech bowed its gleaming head and disappeared back into the kitchen.

Although I couldn't quite identify what was on the plate in front of me, it did smell good. I picked up my fork, hesitating.

"It is Zhore food," Sarzhin offered, "but I chose something close to a human dish. You would perhaps call it crepes and mushrooms on Gaia. I grow the fungi here myself. I shall show you after breakfast."

Fungi didn't sound particularly appetizing, but I knew they were considered a delicacy back on Gaia. My family had never bothered with anything beyond the basics, although my father had set up a little hydroponic farm in a utility shed behind the house where we grew tomatoes and squash to supplement the bland rations that formed the bulk of our diet.

"Great," I said, more because it seemed he expected a response than because I thought mushrooms sounded great…or, for that matter, because I was interested in seeing where he grew them. Besides, I had slept so late that this breakfast was almost a lunch, and I was hungry. Then

I forced myself to put the forkful of crepe and fungus in my mouth.

The rich taste of butter and something more subtle, more savory, seemed to explode over my taste buds. I'd had real butter exactly three times in my life, but it had left such an indelible impression that I had no trouble recognizing it now. I quickly took up another forkful, and then another.

"Good?" asked Sarzhin. He sounded almost amused.

At least I remembered to swallow before I replied, "Amazing."

"Excellent."

He applied himself to his own plate. Any thoughts I'd had of sneaking a look at him while he was eating vanished; his hood still drooped so low that I could see nothing of his face, only the fork disappearing up into the recesses of the bulky fabric and then reappearing quite clean. I found myself wondering whether Zhores used forks back on their home world or if the utensil was a concession to my human ways.

After a moment he said, "You are currently enrolled in university coursework, are you not?"

"Yes." Why should he care?

"You will continue with that. I will have a desktop unit installed in your room. Is there anything else you require?"

My freedom, I thought, but I only shook my head. "All my books are already on my tablet. But—you really want me to keep going to school?"

"Of course," he replied, as if surprised that I should have even asked the question. "I wish your life to be disrupted as little as possible."

Funny sentiment for someone who had basically blackmailed me into being here in the first place. I just murmured, "Thanks," and went back to eating. That seemed to be the safest thing to do.

He seemed to guess my mood, and went on with his own breakfast. The rest of the meal passed in silence. The mech came in to clear away our empty plates, and Sarzhin rose from his seat.

"Come," he said. "Let me show you something of where you'll be living."

The mansion seemed almost bigger on the inside than it appeared from the outside, if that were possible. Why one person needed all that space, I couldn't imagine, although I had to admit to myself there was something quite decadent about having room after room, each devoted to its own purpose—the library, which had real books on the shelves, in languages both human and alien; the Zhore's study, with banks of gleaming screens and yet more books; a gallery filled with art from a dozen worlds, some of it quite hideous to my untrained eyes; the kitchen and the ranks of bedrooms and bathrooms. He did not show me his chambers, however.

"And the greenhouse," he said finally, after he had taken me all over the house and I had begun to feel as if I could do with another plate of those marvelous crepes and mushrooms.

The space was huge, easily the size of my parents' entire homestead. Far above us was a many-paned ceiling of clear polymer. Grow lights in various spectrums hung from metal bars separating the polymer panes, and all around us were plants in so many shapes and sizes and colors that I didn't quite know where to look first.

"Azar lilies," he told me, pointing out a row of elegant blooms in shades of deep blood red to almost black. "Highly prized."

"They are?" I asked stupidly, then blushed. I probably should have known that, but besides helping my father with his hydroponics, botany wasn't very high on my list of priorities.

The dark hood tilted down toward me. "I just sold a particularly fine specimen to the chairman of your Gaian Relocation Corporation for ten thousand units."

"Ten thousand?" I gasped. "For a flower?"

"Oh, yes."

Well, that explained where he got some of his money, I supposed. The source of the Zhore's wealth had been the subject of some idle speculation between Libba and myself, back in the days when we still discussed such things, but I'd never imagined he was selling flowers for more apiece than it had cost my sister to go to college.

He did seem quite proud of the greenhouse, and I was forced to admit it was pretty spectacular, with its careful sections of rare flowers and exotic vegetables. The fungi sprouted from a variety of wooden stumps or trays of mossy-looking substances, back in a far corner where none of the grow lights had been hung. Some of the mushrooms looked a little frightening in their natural state; I was glad they had come out of the kitchen already prepared so I didn't have a chance to be scared off from eating them.

At length we returned to the dining room, where the mech fed us another amazing meal—this one a very fine casserole with vegetables that had to have come from the greenhouse, as well as tender meat cutlets whose origin I didn't recognize. No huge surprise, as my family couldn't afford real meat. Most people on Lathvin IV couldn't, except executives with the GRC. We mostly ate soy substitutes and used protein capsules as supplements.

Sarzhin told me the cutlets were more mushrooms. Not that I was an expert, since I'd had meat only twice in my life, both times when my family still lived on the moon, but the texture and taste reminded me of my last birthday meal there, when I'd had something called a tenderloin.

I must have made a surprised sound.

He said quietly, "The Zhore are what your people would call vegetarians."

"Oh," I responded, since I didn't know what else to say. You could have said the same thing about most of the people I knew, although they didn't really keep to that sort of diet by choice.

After that we ate in silence for awhile until the mech showed up to clear the table, although Sarzhin seemed in no hurry to rise from his seat. I remained in my place and fought back a yawn. We'd had wine with dinner, just one glass apiece, but I wasn't used to even that much. I'd drunk

champagne on my eighteenth birthday and had tasted
something called retsina once and thought it quite nasty,
but that was about it for my experiences with alcohol.

Sarzhin's hooded head turned toward me. "You
asked me last night what my purpose was in bringing you
here." He paused, then went on, "Anika, I must ask you
something."

I sat up a little straighter in my chair, the after-dinner
lassitude abruptly disappearing at the intensity I heard in
his voice. Throughout the day he had been unfailingly
polite, so much so that for quite large spans—well, at least
five or ten minutes at a stretch—I had almost forgotten to
be afraid of him. But now my heart began to beat a little
more quickly, and I knotted my fingers into the napkin in
my lap.

Silent, I stared back at him, at the concealing hood, at
the gloved fingers that lay black against black on the shining tabletop. He had six fingers on each hand, I realized.

"Anika, will you marry me?"

The words were simple enough, but at first I couldn't
quite comprehend their meaning. Surely this person—
this alien—hadn't just asked me to be his wife!

It seemed, though, that he had. I gaped at him, the
dinner I had just eaten beginning to churn in my stomach.

"You may answer without fear," he said, his deep
voice quiet and calm. "No harm will ever come to you in
this house, or by my hand."

Fine words. Then again, he had said or done nothing throughout the day that could possibly be construed

as threatening. Which didn't mean much, of course, as I knew nothing of him or his race. He could be lying about not hurting me. Somehow that didn't matter. I knew I couldn't possibly accept his preposterous proposal—even if he hadn't blackmailed me into being here, surely he couldn't expect a human woman to readily agree to be his wife?

"I can't marry you," I said at once. This had to be a bad dream. Visions from horror vids past rose up in my mind, which seemed all too eager to present a series of gruesome possibilities as to what might be hiding under that hooded cloak. Was marriage the same for the Zhore as it was for humans? Would he expect me to—to—

His fingers clenched against the tabletop. I swallowed against the sour bile in my throat before I added, "I don't even know you. And besides, you're a—a—"

"A Zhore?" he interjected. "True enough. I will not dispute you on that point." He pushed his chair back; metal screeched against the polished stone floor, and I winced. "It is late. We will end our day now, I think."

That sounded like a wonderful idea. Too bad he hadn't decided to end the discussion about five minutes earlier. I got up as well. "I'll just go to my room now."

"You know the way?"

"Oh, yes," I said quickly. The last thing I wanted was for him to follow me upstairs. "Thank you. That is, thank you for dinner and for the tour of your home."

"It is your home now as well."

Yes, I supposed it was. My home...or my prison. I

only nodded and threw a tentative little smile in his direction that probably would have fooled no one, even an alien. And I fled to my room.

Not that I felt particularly safe there, either. He made no move to follow me, though, and that was something. I locked the door, stumbled over to the bed, and sank down on it, then hugged my trembling hands against myself.

This was the reason Sarzhin had demanded that my father send me to him? Because he wanted a wife?

I couldn't begin to fathom it. He was an alien. If he wanted a spouse, a companion in this huge house, why didn't he get one among his own kind? Or, if that were somehow impossible, why couldn't he have just bought himself a wife from one of those dubious sectors whose business it was to handle such transactions?

Good questions. I didn't think I had the courage to ask them of Sarzhin, however.

Instead, I got up and checked the door. It was locked. Not that that meant much; I guessed the Zhore could get in if he really wanted to. Could come in and—

No, I was not going to think of such things. True, he had bent my brain about fifty different ways with his shocking request, but he had made no move to touch me, done nothing to prevent me from all but running away from him. That had to mean something.

What that might be, I wasn't quite sure of at the moment. I did know that pacing around the room and compulsively checking the lock every five minutes wasn't going to do me much good. Somehow I made myself go into the bathroom and wash my face and clean my teeth with the ultrasonic device he'd provided for me. I got out of my dingy gray coveralls and into my equally utilitarian sleep shirt and slid into that seductively soft bed.

It must have been the bed, because at length I did manage to fall asleep. A fitful sleep, though, broken by the passing brush of nightmares. More than once my eyes opened and strained against the darkness, looking for the deeper black of Sarzhin's robes.

I never saw him, of course.

The next morning, Sarzhin acted as if nothing odd had passed between us the night before, so I followed his lead and attempted to do the same. It actually wasn't as difficult as I had feared, because he spoke of my computer and my schoolwork, and I responded in kind. In fact, the computer appeared later that morning, brought by a too obviously curious delivery man I vaguely recognized as one of the odd-jobbers who hung around the Port Natchez commissary. He didn't get much more than a quick peek inside, though, before the mech briskly took the white plastic box from him and shut the door in his face. A second or two later I heard the airlock cycle and knew the man must have left.

Getting the computer configured and my coursework loaded onto it took a good deal of the remainder of the day. To be sure, I took longer at the task than I really needed to. Anything to avoid being alone in the Zhore's company.

Luckily, Sarzhin made himself scarce. Maybe he was off tending his lilies, hoping he'd earn back what he'd spent on the computer. No, that was silly. The computer was top of the line, or at least top of the limited line the Port Natchez commissary carried, but you still could have bought ten of them for what that crazy executive had paid for his one plant.

Late in the afternoon, though, a diffident knock came at my door. I opened it to see Sarzhin standing there.

"You have gotten the setup working?"

"Yes," I replied. I hated to invite him into my room, but I thought it would be rude not to let him see that I had everything up and running. So I pointed at the table where I'd had the mech deposit the computer. "It went pretty flawlessly. I just finished downloading yesterday's lectures. I'm a little bit behind, but I'll get caught up tomorrow."

"I apologize for the disruption."

I almost said that it was no problem, but the truth was, I wouldn't have gotten behind if I hadn't come here. So I shrugged. "I work fast. I told my instructors I'd just moved. They understood."

He nodded, then seemed to hesitate as he gazed down at me. "Dinner will be served soon." Another one of those odd little pauses, and he said, "You did not bring many belongings with you."

At first I didn't quite understand what he meant, but then I looked down at myself, at the baggy coveralls

I wore, and realized he was saying, in the most oblique way possible, that my wardrobe was not quite up to snuff, either in variety or design. True, these coveralls were more a dark khaki rather than the gray I'd worn the day before, but that was really splitting hairs.

"I brought what I had," I said honestly. "I'm sorry I don't match your fancy house."

He drew himself up, and somehow I sensed he had tensed beneath the enveloping robes. "I did not mean to offend you."

"No offense. As my father always says, there's no shame in being poor, but it can be damned inconvenient."

A laugh drifted out of the hood. Funny that an alien could make such a human sound. Actually, his voice sounded very human as well. If I listened hard, I could hear just the faintest hint of some sort of accent around the edges of his pronunciation, but really, most of the time he sounded as polished as a commentator on a 'net program. He lifted one gloved hand and extended it, a thin piece of metallic-coated plastic held between his thumb and forefinger. "Take this, then."

"What is it?"

"You've never seen a credit voucher?"

I shook my head. My parents handled all the money matters in the household. The local currency of Port Natchez was largely barter. I'd earned spare components for our atmospheric generator by trading a few hours in someone's hydroponic garden or babysitting a couple of the settlers' kids, but that was about it.

"You will purchase yourself an adequate wardrobe."

"I couldn't—"

"Yes, you will." Before I could flinch or pull my hand back, he reached out and slid the plastic voucher into my unwilling palm. It felt cool and hard against my skin.

"But—"

"Return that to me, when you are done with it," he said smoothly, overriding my protests as if he hadn't heard them. "Dinner will be at nineteen hundred. You have approximately one half-hour."

I didn't know him very well, but usually when someone adopts such a firm tone, it means they really don't want to be argued with. Any further debate would most likely be pointless, so I just nodded. If he wanted to waste his money, that was his problem.

The hood dipped slightly, as if he had nodded. "One half-hour," he repeated, and then he turned and left.

That didn't give me a huge amount of time, considering the fact that I basically knew nothing about clothes, either where to get them or what was even supposed to be in fashion. All our clothing came from the Port Natchez commissary, which carried a decent supply of coveralls and other work wear, outer and underwear, and sturdy shoes, but would probably be considered somewhat lacking in the style department. Ordering items from out of the system didn't seem to be a viable option, either, as they would take forever to get here and the shipping costs would most likely be higher than the actual pieces themselves. However, Lathvin did have two moons, one of which had a fairly large spaceport complex of its own. The system was located in a strategic spot for refueling, and so served as something of a shipping and transport hub. A good deal of traffic that had nothing to do with the homesteaders and the development of the planet itself passed in and out of the moon, and I recalled Libba mentioning in one of her messages that there had been a sizable duty-free shopping area in the spaceport.

So I went to my computer and did a little investigating, and found that some of the shops actually would deliver down to the planet's surface for what seemed like a reasonable fee. Of course, I had no idea what was fashionable and what wasn't, but I guessed I probably wouldn't need fancy dresses or shoes with heels so high I couldn't imagine ever trying to walk in them. However, combinations of fitted tunics with slim pants seemed very popular, so I ordered a bunch of those in various colors and necklines, as well as some pretty flat shoes that were shown in the images accompanying those outfits.

Despite my worries over doing significant damage to Sarzhin's credit voucher, in the end the total wasn't as bad as I had thought. The clothing would be delivered some time the next day, so he'd just have to live with my dingy coveralls for one more evening.

I did go into the bathroom and brush my hair and apply some of the tinted lip moisturizer I'd found in one of the drawers there. How the Zhore would have even known that human women used such things, I wasn't really sure, but the 'cycled air could be drying, even as damp as the planet was overall. Lotions and moisturizers were pretty much considered necessities on Lathvin, along with vitamin supplements and rainproof boots. You couldn't really call the lip tint makeup, especially when contrasted with the professionally painted women I'd just seen in the spaceport shops' catalogs, but I still shook my head at myself. Would a Zhore even notice the difference between brushed and unbrushed hair, or care if my lips were now a slightly deeper pink?

Probably his comment about my clothing had bothered me more than I thought it had. I'd never had the time or inclination to think about my appearance and didn't know why he should care about it, either.

Well, except for the fact that he apparently wanted to marry me.

I shivered a little and wondered if he would ask me again tonight. Whether he did or didn't wouldn't change the fact that he was expecting me, and that now, judging by the chronometer on the wall above my desk, I was already five minutes late.

I shut the bathroom door and went downstairs to meet him.

He asked if I had taken care of my shopping, and I told him that I had, and that the packages should be delivered tomorrow. He nodded, apparently satisfied by my reply.

"And here's your voucher," I said, sliding it across the gleaming tabletop toward him. That way, I didn't have to hand it to him directly and risk brushing my hand against his.

Slim black-gloved fingers wrapped around the plastic and lifted it. Without speaking, he took the voucher and slipped it away somewhere within the folds of his robes.

The silence seemed to stretch, filled with unspoken tension. Maybe I had offended him by so obviously trying to avoid his touch.

"How are your lilies?" I blurted.

"They are very well, thank you," he said.

Before then I'd never really stopped to think how difficult it could be to carry on a conversation with someone whose face was completely obscured. He could have been smiling at me, or frowning. I didn't know, and as his tone remained calm and level, I couldn't discern anything from that, either. True, it was entirely possible the Zhore didn't share any facial expressions with humans, and I wouldn't have been able to tell anything even if I had been able to see him clearly.

That he was humanoid in shape was clear enough, even with the concealing cloak. So far the Gaian Federation had encountered nine sentient alien races; of those, five were humanoid—some so close to humans in their physiognomy that debates were ongoing about convergent evolution or "space seeding" by some highly developed race some time in the remote past. I didn't know if the Zhore fell into that category or not, as no one had ever seen one, but they were still classified as humanoid since they had two arms, two legs, and one head. Maybe that should have reassured me, but humanoid still was not human.

Then Sarzhin seemed to take pity on me, or possibly he didn't like the silence too much, because he asked if I was catching up all right with my coursework. Relieved, I told him about the vid-lectures I'd watched and the paper I'd begun to write on the original Gaian-Eridani trade agreements.

I didn't know if he was really interested or not, but he gave a good enough imitation of attention, and the prosy topic was enough to keep the conversation going throughout most of our meal. Actually, he made a few suggestions as to further areas I might research, and I gratefully accepted his advice. If nothing else, he clearly was well-read. Zhore didn't attend any of the universities the other humanoids had set up and now shared, but of course they must have their own institutions on their home world—which, like the Zhore, no one had ever seen. They allowed outsiders as far in as the fifth planet from their sun, but their own world, the fourth one in the Zhore system, was off-limits to outsiders.

Despite our warlike past, we Gaians are more interested in exploration and peaceful settlement, and we respected the Zhores' boundaries. We hadn't done the same here on Lathvin, but then again, it wasn't their home world. Anyway, disputes still raged as to which race had really set foot on the planet first.

Dinner—another excellent meal, this time some kind of grain and vegetable dish—wound down, and the mech once again appeared to clear away our dishes.

Sarzhin sat up a little straighter in his chair and said, "Anika, will you marry me?"

This time the request wasn't quite as unexpected, but I still shivered a little as I heard his deep, solemn voice utter those words. I stared down at the black, polished surface of the dining room table. "You know I can't."

"Do I?" He sounded almost amused.

"Look, even if you weren't—I mean, even if you were a human man, I wouldn't marry you."

"Why not?"

I knew he wasn't that obtuse, no, not by a long shot. But if he really wanted it spelled out for him… "Because I've known you for what, a day and a half? I know nothing of you, and you know nothing of me. How can you make a marriage out of that?"

"And that is your only objection? Not the fact that I am a Zhore?"

How was I supposed to answer that? If someone had put the question to me in a purely hypothetical manner, I probably would have said I didn't have any objection to such a thing in principle. After all, members of the different humanoid races did intermarry from time to time, although in some cultures those liaisons were frowned upon. I'd teased Libba once or twice about bringing home a purple-skinned, antennaed Eridani boyfriend from the university, but I knew she was too conventional for such a thing. My father had joined in, saying he didn't care if her boyfriend was purple or covered in fur, as long as he had a real job. At that point she'd blushed and switched off the transmission.

But it was one thing to espouse such an admittedly liberal viewpoint in a theoretical sense and quite another to be confronted by it in your own life. Also, at least I knew what an Eridani looked like. I couldn't say the same thing about a Zhore. Sarzhin could be hiding anything under that cloak—horns, tentacles, fangs.

"All right, it's one of my main objections," I said.

He chuckled. "At least you are honest. I will say that I do appreciate that. My people have little patience for dishonesty."

No wonder they're not big fans of the GRC. Since he sounded at least a little approving and not that disappointed, I felt brave enough to ask, "Why are you asking me, anyway? Wouldn't it make more sense to marry a Zhore woman?"

A sudden stillness around him told me that I had just asked exactly the wrong question. An uneasy silence fell, and I quickly redirected my attention toward the dark tabletop once more.

"I cannot answer that question," he replied at length. His voice was cold and even, all approval gone. "At least, not in a way you could possibly understand."

That sounded almost insulting, but I decided not to press the point. Obviously I had struck some sort of nerve. As this was his house, and his rules, I decided it would be better to keep my mouth shut. So far he had been nothing but courteous to me, but that didn't mean much. I didn't know what a Zhore might be capable of, although no one in Port Natchez had ever said anything bad about Sarzhin or the others of his kind who lived in our region. The worst anyone could say was that the Zhore kept to themselves.

I said, "I'm sorry. I didn't mean to offend you. It's just that we know so little of your people—"

"No offense taken," he said at once. "It is a...difficult...topic. Perhaps at some point I can attempt to explain it to you. For now, however, I think it best that you go to bed."

I was far from sleepy, but I only nodded. It would be a relief to escape to my room, where I could shut the door and try to pretend I wasn't sharing a house with an enigmatic alien who wanted to make me his wife. I rose from my chair, and he added, "You are free to communicate with your family. I would guess they are concerned for your safety. I merely ask that the mails you send be text only—no video. And please, do not speak with them of what I have asked of you."

Startled, I glanced over at him. He had remained seated—the hood was tilted up slightly toward me, but of course I still saw nothing of his face. Earlier in the day I had thought of trying to contact my parents, but I worried that he was monitoring or intercepting everything I sent from my new computer and thought it probably better to do nothing. Now that I had Sarzhin's express permission, I could send a message to my parents and let them know I was fine. Well, mostly fine, anyway. They didn't need to know what my host's marriage requests were doing to my already shaky peace of mind.

"Sure." I didn't bother to add that I wouldn't have

spoken of it even if he had told me it was all right. I didn't even want to imagine my father's reaction if he learned what the Zhore had really wanted of me. "I understand."

Actually, I didn't understand at all, but at the moment I only wanted to get away.

He said, "Thank you."

I took that as my opportunity to end the conversation. I managed to smile and then left him, still seated at the head of that enormous table. Somehow I kept myself from turning to look back at him. How many nights had he spent sitting alone in that dining room before I had come here to stay?

It shouldn't have mattered. Somehow, though, as I mounted the stairs to my room, I kept seeing that enigmatic black figure, and the echoing expanses of the empty chamber around him. A little tremor of doubt went through me. It can't have been easy, rattling around in this enormous house by himself.

And that shouldn't be your problem, I told myself, and shut my bedroom door behind me. *Even though he's tried to make it your problem.*

True, of course, but I couldn't shake the feeling there was something else I could have said, something that would have made my exit less abrupt. After all, he had just granted me permission to communicate with my family, and I hadn't even thanked him.

Since it was too late for me to do anything about that, I just went to the computer and pulled up my mail client. I needed to compose a message that sounded cheerful and yet not too effusive. I'd never been the type to gush, and my father would be sure to notice something odd if I waxed too rhapsodic about my current living situation.

I'm all settled in, and the Zhore—I wondered whether it was all right to give my parents my host's name, and then decided against it—*has done everything he can to make sure I'm comfortable. I have a nice room of my own, and I also have my own computer setup, so there are no worries about me continuing with my university coursework. He was adamant that I not miss out on any of that. The house is quite nice, and he has a greenhouse with all sorts of interesting plants. Everything is going well. I just wanted to let you know I'm all right. I miss you, but you don't need to worry about me. Let me know how your new hydroponic setup is working out. Love, Anika.*

Before I could erase the whole thing and start over, I hit the "send" button and let the mail fly off into the ether. How my parents would react to the stilted little missive, I couldn't begin to guess. After all, since it was straight text and not video, they had no way of knowing I hadn't written the whole thing with a particle gun pressed against my temple, or even whether I'd written it myself. Well, maybe my little request at the end about my father's hydroponic experiments would help to clue them in that I really was the author.

Afterward, I went to bed. I suppose I was more tired than I had thought, because I ended up falling asleep quite soon after I lay down—but not soon enough to keep me from wondering what it would be like to have that dark shape lying next to me, that deep voice the last thing I heard before I shut my eyes.

I shivered, even though the bed coverings were soft and warm.

The next morning I found a breakfast tray outside my room. It could have been a signal of Sarzhin's displeasure with me, or possibly just a sign that he had other business to attend to and didn't have time for a leisurely breakfast. I tried to tell myself the little stab of disappointment that passed through me was simply because the meal on the tray—a warm, sweet grain dish and some fruit—wasn't nearly as interesting as the two other breakfasts I had shared with him.

That disappointment didn't last long, however, because soon afterward the mech appeared at my door carrying a large box, which proved to be my clothing purchases of the day before. Although I knew I should get back to the paper I was writing and the lectures that were undoubtedly queuing up in my downloads folder, I spent the good part of an hour pulling out all the outfits, arranging the shoes, deciding which one of them I should wear first. I hoped I could be forgiven for acting like a girl. After all, I'd never had the opportunity to wear pretty things before. I hadn't realized that clothes could feel as wonderful as they looked—the elegant fabrics whispered over my fingertips and clung to my form in a way my utilitarian work garments never had.

It was difficult to choose which to wear first, but I decided at last on a dark greenish-blue outfit with bronze-colored embroidery around the neckline. The girl who stared out at me from the mirror seemed almost a stranger, elegant and refined, certainly not someone who had once been up to her elbows in oil helping her father repair a broken pump in the atmospheric generator.

In that moment I was glad I had decided against cutting my hair. A few months earlier I had almost chopped it all off because all I ever did was braid it back to keep it out of the way, but at the last minute I'd put down the scissors, reluctant to get rid of it even if it wasn't as pretty as my sister's red-gold waves. Now, with it lying loose over my shoulders, the warm brown looked sleek and rich against the deep color of my tunic, and not drab at all.

Of course, it didn't seem as if I'd have much opportunity to show myself off, as I received no summons to go downstairs and therefore returned to my computer with some reluctance. Through sheer effort of will I pounded through the first draft of my paper on the Eridani-Gaian trade agreement, and then paused to see if I'd gotten any mail. My father had just responded to my message; he tended to check his own mail in the middle of the day when he took a break to eat.

We're very happy to hear that you're safe and doing well and that you're continuing with your schoolwork. Has the Zhore said anything to you about why he wants you there?

Typical of my father to ask questions to which I had

no answers…at least no answers I wanted to give. I had no idea what I could possibly say, so I closed the message and told myself I'd answer him later, when I had more time to think. In the meantime, I had a lecture I needed to watch and take notes on, because the follow-up study group had been scheduled for very early the next morning. That was one problem with doing these things remotely—the professors tried to rotate the live-feed study groups so no one person was always stuck with the shift in the middle of the night, but the upshot was that sooner or later you'd be staggering into a study group at three o'clock in the morning local time.

I'd gotten through approximately fifteen minutes of the xenolinguistics lecture when I heard a knock. After pausing the feed, I got up from my chair and opened the door.

Sarzhin's dark, hooded form waited outside. Absurdly, a little rush of excitement went through me. At least it appeared I wasn't going to be eating lunch off a tray in my room.

"My apologies for not sharing breakfast," he said. "I had business to attend to."

"That's fine," I replied, and chided myself mentally for sounding a little too breathless. "I was studying."

"Are you hungry now?"

"Oh, yes. Trade agreements can do that to a girl, I guess."

He chuckled. "Well, we must do something about that."

I stepped out through the doorway and turned to palm the lock. When I faced back out into the corridor,

I saw Sarzhin standing there, staring at me. At least, I assumed that was what he was doing—the hood had tilted down toward me, and he made no sign of moving.

"Is something wrong?"

At once the hood jerked upright. "No—that is, I should have said you were looking very well. Your new things arrived this morning?"

"Yes." I quelled the urge to turn around so he could see my finery from all angles. "Better?"

"Much better."

It wasn't hard to hear the approval in his tone, and a little heat flooded my cheeks. I glanced away, hoping that the Zhore wasn't very good at reading human reactions and so therefore would have no idea what my sudden flush meant.

He continued, the words sounding a little rushed, "I thought we might try something a little different today."

"Different?" I wasn't sure I liked the sound of that. I'd barely gotten used to the bit of a routine we'd put in place so far.

"You'll see. Come."

And so I followed him downstairs, past the dining room. I could feel myself frowning in puzzlement, but I continued to trot along behind him as he swept on to the back of the mansion and the entrance to the greenhouse.

In the main part of the house I'd hardly been able to hear the rain, but here the sound of it was more pronounced, the raindrops creating a dull roar as they hit the heavy polymer panels overhead. Somehow, though, the noise didn't intrude, but created instead a soothing background note, rather like a recording I'd heard once of waves breaking against a seashore. The air was warm and heavy, filled with the scents of hundreds of exotic flowers.

"Here," Sarzhin said, and I looked to see that a small table and two chairs had been set up in a little artificial glade created by a dozen or so small specimen trees in their individual tubs. A glow cell flickered from a faceted glass holder at the center of the table, while our meals appeared to be already waiting for us under protective clear globes.

In all, it was very lovely, and quite a change from the elegant but cold dining room where we'd previously shared our meals. Of course I immediately wondered whether he'd set all this up because he thought it would provide a setting more conducive to my accepting his proposal, but I tried to tell myself this was only lunch, and the previous two days he had waited until after dinner to ask me to marry him. A small reassurance, but at the moment I was willing to take what I could get.

"This really is different," I told him.

"You like it?"

About that at least I could be honest. "Very much."

He indicated I should sit down, so I took my seat in the little chair of delicately wrought metal situated opposite his. After I had seated myself, he sat across from me and poured some water into my glass from a pitcher that had been sitting off to one side of the table. I had gotten quite fond of that water during my short time in the

Zhore's home. Unlike the water back at the homestead, which always had a faintly metallic taste from being processed and reprocessed, the water here was sweet and pure and refreshed me in a way that our 'cycled water never could.

"Does it remind you of your home world?" he inquired, as he lifted the covers from our plates and set them aside on a second, smaller table that had been placed a few feet off, apparently for serving duties.

"Gaia?"

He nodded.

"I wouldn't know," I replied. As usual, I had no idea what was on my plate, but it smelled delicious. Somehow I kept myself from lifting my fork and plowing right into the food. I guessed I should answer Sarzhin's question before I started stuffing my face. "That is, I was born on Gaia, but my parents moved to the moon when I was only eighteen standard months old. I don't remember anything about Gaia."

"Oh. Pity."

I supposed it was. Twenty years before I was born, no one would have attempted such a thing with a child that age, but once the gravity compensators were perfected, living on the moon didn't have the same physiological drawbacks that it used to. Still, it had been odd to see Gaia's blue-green shape rise and fall in the sky and know I'd probably never get back there. Even that expense, small as it was, didn't fit into my parents' budget, especially since neither of them had any friends or family for us to visit on

Gaia. The only reason we made it out to Lathvin was that the GRC pays full passage to its homestead planets. If you want to leave, the cost is on you, but getting there isn't a problem. And Libba's fare to Eridani had been included in her scholarship funds, but she certainly didn't have any left over for return trips, which was why we hadn't seen her for almost five years.

"What about your world?" I asked, and popped a forkful of something rich and savory into my mouth.

"It resembles some parts of it, perhaps." He lifted his water glass and drank. "These plants have been gathered from a dozen worlds, any that support a Gaia-class atmosphere."

That was the standard designation for a world where humanoids could breathe the air without assistance, but it still seemed a little odd to hear an alien use such a Gaia-centric term. Privately, I'd thought for some years that it was the height of arrogance to land on an alien world and try to transmute its atmosphere into something it wasn't, but I'd known better than to utter such heresy in my parents' home. Anyway, the Zhore didn't appear to share my scruples, as they were here terraforming Lathvin IV right along with us humans. At least this scrubby little planet didn't have any indigenous sentient life, and barely any animal—a few rock borers that lived beneath the surface, some insects that probably no one except the xeno-entomologists would miss. And its plant species could be counted on the fingers of two hands…even if you were a twelve-fingered Zhore.

"It almost feels like we're outside," I ventured. "That is, outside someplace where you can sit and not asphyxiate."

"You've never experienced that, have you? To live on a world whose environment isn't inimical, where it's safe and even desirable to walk around on the surface without protective gear?"

"No," I said, and set down my fork. Some would say you couldn't miss what you never had, but somehow his words awoke a wistful longing in me, a desire to know what it would be like to walk outside and lift my head to the sky and the wind and not have to worry about breathing apparatus or a containment suit. "Have you?"

"Of course. Zhoraan never suffered the same ecological disasters as Gaia—it is a world of great natural beauty."

Zhoraan, I repeated silently. To my knowledge, no one had ever learned the name of the Zhore home world, just as no outlander had ever been allowed to set foot there. Since I had the notion that Sarzhin did very little by chance, he must have given me his world's name as a gift, perhaps something to further establish trust between us.

"Do you miss it?"

"No."

Startled, I gazed across the table at him, at the obscuring cloak and low-falling hood. Not for the first time I wished I could see something of his expression, even if I might not have been able to read it very well. "Really? Even though it's so beautiful?"

His voice level, he replied, "Why should I? I have everything I need here."

Again I found myself flushing, so I busied myself with drinking some more water and then having another mouthful of the delicious whatever-it-was. But that only lasted so long, and since he didn't seem inclined to say anything else, I knew I'd have to come up with some sort of reply. "You're a better person than I am. I've never liked this planet."

"Indeed?"

"Indeed. Oh, some days I could almost convince myself that I didn't totally hate it, but..." I trailed off and sighed. "Really, it doesn't have a lot to recommend it, except that it's got gravity and other surface conditions in the habitable range. I suppose by the time I'm an old woman it'll be really livable, but right now it's just damp, dark, and pretty darn inconvenient."

He laughed then, a rich amused laugh that somehow made me think of the dark chocolate bars my father used to get for Libba and me as holiday presents. "When you put it that way, I suppose I can see your point. And of course I would assume that your life as a homesteader would be rather different from the one I live here."

"Just a little." Yes, he had two atmospheric generators on the property, but I'd never seen him do anything to maintain them. That was probably part of the mech's duties, I supposed—the generators were supposed to run pretty much unattended, in theory. But that theory didn't cover substandard replacement parts or filters which clogged up or flat out rusted, and so babysitting the generators became pretty much a full-time job for most of the homesteaders. Because if your generator didn't produce its quota in a given month, then somebody from the Atmospheric Development Agency came by, and the next thing you knew you'd been given a fine that would postpone your payoff date for the homestead by a good two or three standard months.

I somehow guessed Sarzhin didn't have to deal with anything so mundane. I added, "Don't mind me. I'm sure my feelings about Lathvin are probably more jealousy than anything else."

"Jealousy?"

"Because my sister got to go to college on Eridani, and I got stuck here. Oh, she got a full scholarship, and probably I could have if I'd tried for one, but there are always odds and ends that a scholarship doesn't cover, and my parents just couldn't afford to send me off-world, too. So here I am."

It somehow seemed too intimate to add that I'd felt I would be abandoning my parents to manage the homestead on their own if I'd applied for a scholarship and left them behind the way Libba had. Yes, I'd left them behind to come here, but five kilometers' worth of separation was a far different thing from five hundred light-years.

"Yes, here you are." He was silent for a moment. I could somehow tell he was watching me intently from within the confines of that dark hood, and I did my best not to blink or look away. "I hope you will forgive me if

I say I am very glad that you were, as you put it, 'stuck here.'"

That makes one of us, I thought, but of course I didn't say it aloud. For one thing, it certainly wasn't his fault that I hadn't been able to get away from Lathvin IV, and second of all, he had done his best to make my time here in his home as comfortable as possible. Besides the dreaded marriage proposals, of course.

I smiled at him, since that seemed to be the best reply I could come up with. Perhaps noticing my awkwardness, he went on to talk about the trees surrounding us, and how he had worked very hard on the greenhouse setup so it could provide micro-climates for the dizzying variety of plants he grew there. It actually was very interesting, and I found myself gaining new respect for him, for the determination that drove him to create this little piece of paradise hidden away from the rest of the world. I would be lying, however, if I didn't say I was more than a little relieved when our lunch ended with nary a proposal of marriage in sight. So perhaps he really did reserve those for the conclusion of our evening meals.

At any rate, he let me go back to my room afterward with no protest. I actually did have more studying to do, and he seemed to accept my explanation for how I needed to spend the rest of the afternoon. He said he would see me at dinner, and left it at that. An importunate suitor, he was not. Maybe he thought he had plenty of time. After all, there had been no discussion of how long my tenure here was supposed to be.

I didn't want to think about why he had left the whole situation so open-ended.

Another day passed, and then another. We fell into a regular routine, sharing meals more often than not. Dinner, however, was sacrosanct, as was the inevitable question at its end. And every night I had to answer no.

It wasn't that I disliked the Zhore, or even resented him all that much for compelling me to take up residence in his house. If I were forced to admit it, well, my life here was much easier than it had been in my parents' homestead. True, if given my choice, of course I would have returned home, but it wasn't as if he had locked me up in a dungeon or something—not that any could have even existed on Lathvin IV, given the planet's high water table. But of course it was impossible that I could consider becoming Sarzhin's wife, not when I had never even seen his face.

I worked hard at my studies, as much because I didn't want to fail my parents as because it gave me something to fill up my time. And I did do very well, my midterm scores higher than they had been in previous semesters, so obviously all the free time was of some benefit.

All seemed to be going as well as it reasonably could, given the circumstances, but that didn't seem to make much of a difference.

I retired early one night, my latest refusal to Sarzhin still ringing in my ears. As always, he had accepted my demurral with quiet acceptance, but I wondered how long this possibly could go on. By that point I had lived under his roof for a little more than a standard month. Surely he didn't intend to spend the next year listening to me tell him I could never be his wife.

Usually I didn't dream, or at least I had a difficult time remembering my dreams when I awoke the next morning. This time, though, I clearly saw myself wandering through the corridors of Sarzhin's home, even though in my dream it was somehow bigger yet darker than it was in real life. I seemed to be looking for him—I called out his name, but got no reply. Finally, I approached a room I had never seen before, one my dreaming mind told me was his private chamber, although of course I had never seen it with my waking eyes. In a far corner I saw his dark shape, although something in its outline appeared horribly wrong to me. I stepped toward him, and he turned.

The hood was down. And above his shoulders was… nothing. Only a dim space filled with shadows, where his face should be.

I screamed. My eyes snapped open, and I realized I lay in my own bed, with the familiar shapes of my bedroom furniture all around me. Off to one side, the chronograph glowed faintly into the darkness. It was just past two hundred hours.

My breath came as quickly as if I had just spent an unprotected seven minutes outside in Lathvin's inhospitable atmosphere. I sat up in bed, and tried to tell myself that it had only been a dream. A terrible dream, to be sure, but no more real than my dreams of getting off this rock one day.

Shaking, I slid out of bed and went to the bathroom so I could pour myself some water and try to get my disarranged thoughts in order. What had brought on such a dream, after all this time, I had no idea. Surely my time for having nightmares about Sarzhin should have been weeks in the past, back when I didn't know him.

I drank some water, and then splashed some on my face for good measure. Most likely I was just feeling overburdened by schoolwork—I had two papers due by the end of the week. Yes, that had to be it. After all, stress could manifest itself in all sorts of ways, many of them completely illogical.

A soft knock at the door. "Anika? Are you all right?"

How he could have known I had been awakened by a nightmare, I had no idea. I took a deep breath and smoothed my hair down as best I could, then said, "I'm fine, Sarzhin. One moment."

I was far from fine, but I knew I shouldn't leave him waiting out in the hall. After taking another sip or two of water, I went to the door and opened it. Sarzhin waited outside, as black and enigmatic as he had been in my dream. With one important difference, of course—the hood that peered down at me seemed to be quite occupied.

"I heard—that is, I thought you screamed."

"A bad dream," I said at once, even though I

wondered how on earth he could have heard me through a shut door and with who knows how many empty hallways between us. I still had no idea exactly where his chambers lay, although I knew they had to be a good distance off.

"What was it?"

There was no way I could tell him what I had dreamed. "Nothing," I said. "It was silly, really."

"It most certainly didn't sound silly."

No, and it hadn't felt silly at the time. "Our minds play tricks on us," I told him. "That's all. I'm fine now."

He didn't move. "Tell me, Anika."

His voice had a note of quiet command I had never heard before. "I'm sorry I woke you," I said hastily. "Especially for something as stupid as a bad dream. It's nothing—"

"It didn't sound like nothing."

It seemed clear to me that he wasn't about to let this go. I sighed, and crossed my arms. "If you have to know, it was about you."

"I?"

"I dreamed—" Oh, this was ridiculous. "I dreamed I saw you without your hood…and you had no head. I told you it was stupid."

For a long moment he didn't move. Then he reached out and took my hands in his gloved ones. He had always been very careful to avoid touching me, as if he had known I wanted to keep as much distance as possible between us, but now his grip was firm and unhesitating. I didn't dare pull away. Something in his touch told me he did so now only out of necessity.

He raised my hands to his hood and placed them against the heavy fabric. Beneath the rough, slightly nappy material my fingers traced the definite outline of a skull, one more or less of the same proportions as a human's. For a few seconds he held my hands in place, and then he lowered them gently and released his gloved fingers from mine.

"You see?" he said quietly. "I am as real as you are."

That much seemed obvious. I could still feel the shape of his head beneath my fingertips. No horns at least, although I still couldn't comment on the fangs or tentacles. I asked, "Then why do you hide from the world?"

A silence then, one so long I was sure he didn't intend to reply. He let out a little breath and said, "Because I must. Perhaps one day you will understand why."

I wished there were some way I could get him to confide in me. Maybe there was one, actually, but I knew I wouldn't become his wife just to learn his secrets. And yet something in his dark, still shape spoke of a sadness I couldn't begin to understand, one I suddenly wished I might do something to dispel. Surprising myself, I reached out and laid a hand on his forearm. I heard a sudden intake of breath, but I made myself give his arm a gentle squeeze before I let go. He really didn't feel any different from a human — at least, a human who was well-muscled. The flesh under my fingertips had been firm and unyielding.

"I'm sorry I woke you," I said. "But I'm fine. I really need to get back to sleep. That paper—"

"Of course." His normally calm accents sounded a little ruffled to me, but he only went on, "Now that I know you're all right."

"I am."

"Then good night, Anika." He might have nodded; it was difficult to tell in the darkness, which was barely broken by the light of a sconce at quarter-power somewhere down the corridor.

"Good night, Sarzhin." I shut the door and returned to my bed.

But although I had told the Zhore I needed my rest, I lay there for a long time and stared up at the ceiling. Somehow I still felt his gloved hands holding mine, the shape of his head beneath the muffling cloth. It would have been so easy for me to grasp the hood and pull it away, but for some reason he had trusted me not to do such a thing. Truly, the thought hadn't even occurred to me, not until I was lying in bed and replaying the scene in my mind.

What I had done to earn such trust, I didn't know.

He didn't speak of the incident afterward, and so I said nothing, either. From time to time, though, I caught myself watching him out of the corner of my eye, wondering what he would do if I did reach up and push all that concealing fabric away.

What I would see.

Of course I didn't have the courage to do that.

✳

Later that week he asked me if I would like to assist him in the greenhouse.

"It's a worthy occupation," he told me, as the mech cleared away our breakfast plates. "You have said that you've helped your father, and so it seems you already know some of the rudiments of gardening. Would you like to learn more?"

I actually was curious; even the bits and pieces I had picked up so far seemed much more interesting than nursing along a few hydroponic vegetables. If my circumstances had been different, I would have considered how valuable such knowledge would be if I decided to narrow my studies to xeno-botany. Specialists in that area were hot commodities for the GRC's advance reconnaissance teams. But since I had no idea whether Sarzhin intended to ever let me go, I wasn't sure whether acquiring those skills would do much more than help vary my often monotonous days.

It seemed to me, though, that Sarzhin had offered the diversion out of a spirit of generosity, and it would be foolish to turn him down...even though helping out in the greenhouse meant we would be spending far more time together. I didn't know quite how to feel about that.

Speaking quickly, before I could change my mind, I replied, "That sounds wonderful. Thank you, Sarzhin."

"No, thank you."

Even though I couldn't see his face, the warmth in his tone told me how pleased he was. He added, "Shall we?"

I hadn't expected to start so soon, although breakfast was over and I had a light day as far as schoolwork was concerned. Maybe I hesitated, just for a few seconds. But then I said, "Absolutely," and got up from my chair. He rose as well, and led the way back to the greenhouse.

By then it was familiar enough to me—the humid air that somehow managed to be close without cloying, the scents of hundreds of growing things. This time, though, I wouldn't merely be observing the rich plant life, but helping it along, encouraging it to bud and blossom.

"We will start here, I think," Sarzhin told me, pausing in front of a tallish plant in a heavy pot. It had sword-like green leaves and waxy five-petaled flowers. "It is a forgiving specimen, one from a place on Gaia called Hawai'i. Your people call it a plumeria."

A heady, sweet scent, unlike anything I had ever smelled before, seemed to swirl out from the plant. I reached over with one finger to touch a flower's petals, then hesitated. "I won't—I won't hurt it, will I?"

"No. It is quite sturdy, despite its appearance. And easy to propagate as well. Let me show you

He went to the table where his various implements were stored and retrieved a sharp knife from one of the drawers. "Make a cut here," he said, and indicated a spot on one of the gray branches just below where a flower emerged. Then he handed the knife to me.

The knife felt heavy in my hand, even though in

reality it wasn't all that big. I held it awkwardly, hesitating. Intellectually I knew the plant wouldn't start bleeding the second I cut into it, but somehow I couldn't bring myself to lay the blade against the smooth bark.

"Here," Sarzhin said, and reached out to guide my hand to the proper position.

His gloved fingers were warm, the material that covered them as soft and smooth as I remembered. Those fingers wrapped around my hand with a gentle but firm touch, shifting the position of the knife, guiding it to the proper place to cut. And the blade went through the branch without much resistance, the little cutting falling neatly into Sarzhin's other hand.

At once he released me, but the heat of the flesh beneath the supple gloves seemed to linger on my skin. A not entirely unpleasant tingling sensation traveled up my arm. My voice sounded breathless even to me as I asked, "What next?"

He put the branch with its leaves and flower in my hand. "Bring it to the work bench."

I did as he instructed, and then he explained how I should strip off the leaves and set the cutting in a container of dry sand he'd set aside for that purpose. From there it would rest for a few days before being transferred to a pot.

It all seemed simple enough, and from there we moved on to taking more cuttings, this time of a vining plant with dark purple leaves from Epsilon Eridani. That specimen had to be placed immediately in a container filled with a particular blend of nutrients, but the overall procedure was basically the same. Sarzhin only watched as I made the cut, and perversely I found myself almost disappointed that he had not assisted me the way he had with the plumeria. Crazy, considering I'd spent so many days trying to avoid his touch. Now I wanted some kind of excuse to prolong even the brief contact we'd just shared?

"Do you grow them all like this?" I inquired, after I had topped off the vine's slim-necked container of nutrients. "From cuttings, I mean?"

"Not all." He reached up and lifted a plastic bottle from one of the overhead shelves. "Remember to always clean the implements after you're done with them." And he placed the bottle in my left hand, as my right still held the knife. "Fresh rags are in the top drawer."

I set down the knife, looked where he had indicated, and found a pile of synthetic cloths neatly folded in stacks. It was a simple enough procedure to pour some of the disinfecting solution on the knife and wipe it down with a rag, then return it to its own drawer. "So how else do you grow the plants?"

"Some from seed, if I know they will breed true." For some reason he glanced away from me, even though the hood—as ever—hid his expression. "Some come in bulbs and corms, brought here from off-world. And some of those will reproduce as well, if they find the conditions acceptable. But many do best with cuttings. It is not as involved as you might think—I have the databases of fifty worlds to aid me."

It seemed complex enough, but then I was new to anything much more than planting a bunch of tomato and squash seeds in trays and hoping for the best. But obviously Sarzhin knew what he was doing, as all around us were lush reminders of the loving attention he gave every growing thing in his care, from the tiny dwarf succulents of the Stacian deserts to the tall red-leafed trees he'd told me came from the island of Japan on Gaia.

"I'm glad you're showing me," I told him then, and knew as I said the words that they were the simple truth. With some surprise, I glanced down at the chronometer on my wrist and realized we'd spent almost an hour together. The time had gone by so fast I barely realized it was passing.

"It is my pleasure."

The response was something almost anyone would have said, and yet the phrase somehow seemed to resonate in that deep voice of his, imbuing it with far more meaning than the empty pleasantry of a simple human exchange.

Unsure of the best way to respond, I settled for a brief smile, and then mumbled something about having to check my mail to see if one of my professors had gotten back to me regarding a question on my last paper. That was true enough, but it wasn't the real reason why I wanted to go back to my room. His words had been a far cry from the nightly marriage proposal, but somehow in Sarzhin's tone I had heard an echo of the need that underlaid every one of his requests…and I knew there was nothing I could do to fulfill that need.

He nodded, and let me go. I tried to tell myself as I left the greenhouse that I hadn't seen the sudden slump of his shoulders, nor heard the quiet sigh that escaped his lips as I passed, so soft it could have been only the sound of the ventilation system.

But I knew better.

"Anika, will you marry me?"

I closed my eyes, the lingering sweet aftertaste of the wine I had just drunk turning bitter in my mouth. Why did he continue to force the matter? Did he think if he kept at it long enough, somehow he'd chip away at my resolve, a patient river slowly wearing away a stubborn stone?

"You know I can't."

"So you tell me, every evening."

To someone who didn't know him well, his tone might have sounded as calm and even as it always was. I had spent too much time in his company, though, had used too much energy studying the patterns of his voice, since the rise and fall of his tone was the only thing—besides the bits of body language I could glean through the heavy robes—that I really had to give me any clues to what he might be thinking or feeling. Another person wouldn't have heard the edge of tension under those smooth, rounded syllables. His voice was beautiful; I had no idea whether the rest of him was or not.

With an uncharacteristic restlessness, he pushed his wine glass away. At once the mech appeared to remove it.

Sarzhin made an odd little gesture, as if to stop the mech, then shook his head and settled back in his seat.

"Does what I look like matter so much to you?" he asked then. "A spouse's appearance can change—there are accidents, aging. Yet people stay together despite all that."

"But at least they knew what the other person looked like before any of that happened," I protested. "You can't equate the two. And you know appearances don't mean that much to me. I mean, remember the way I looked when I showed up here."

My remark elicited a shake of his head, followed by what sounded like a very unwilling chuckle. "You have a point, I suppose."

That small laugh encouraged me a little, but I guessed from the slump of his shoulders he was still disappointed in me.

For some reason, I was almost disappointed in myself. Maybe someone else would have had the courage to accept him, to give the answer he'd been waiting long weeks to hear. Maybe another woman would have been content with merely knowing what a good companion he could be, how kind and intelligent and everlastingly patient.

For some women—and the disloyal thought that my sister might have been counted among their number passed across my mind—maybe his money would have been enough.

But I wasn't any of those women. True, my tastes in reading and watching vids tended toward adventures and mysteries and the occasional horror tale, if I could manage to hide it from my parents, and not romances. Even so, I'd harbored a few very secret notions of the sort of man I thought I might want to be with one day. Foolish notions, I suppose, of someone tall and handsome, with multiple doctorates and the ability to both pilot a starship and fight off a Stacian sand-serpent single-handedly, but even my admittedly pie-in-the-sky fancies had never extended to a dark-cloaked Zhore whose face I had never seen.

What I didn't really want to admit to myself was that Sarzhin, if you left aside the niggling little detail about him being an alien, was pretty close to ideal, except for the aforementioned sand-snake-fighting talents.

I made myself look at him then. The dark hood was facing toward me, but what he saw, I couldn't say. For all I knew, his eyes were cast upward, to the high windows with the rain continually cascading down them.

"Isn't it enough?" I asked him. "For me to be here with you...helping in the greenhouse, and talking with you over dinner? I really haven't been here all that long, you know. Can't I have more time to...I don't know... think about it?"

He didn't respond at first, but only tilted his head, as if gazing past me to the living artwork of vines and waterfalls that covered the wall behind my chair. A few seconds later he pushed his chair back and rose, then came to stand by my chair. I forced myself to stay where I was, although at all our other dinners he had never made such a movement toward me.

Just the faintest brush of those gloved fingers against a lock of hair as it lay against my shoulder, and he said, "Take all the time you need."

And then he was gone, the black robes flowing around him as he left me sitting there. Another of those odd tremors went through me, and I lifted my own hand to touch that one piece of hair. His fingers hadn't moved it, but mine did. Something like a sharp, stinging twinge seemed to move from that hair to my fingertip, and I jumped. Perhaps it was just an echo of the pain he had felt.

With an abrupt gesture, I pushed all my hair back out of the way and rose out of my seat. I needed to stop acting like an idiot. Sarzhin had granted me some grace. Now I only needed to understand what to do with it.

The next night, when we had finished dinner and the mech had cleared away the plates, the time came for Sarzhin to ask the eventual question...except he didn't. He only hesitated, and watched me from under the hood, and said in questioning tones, "Anika?"

I could only shake my head mutely.

"Ah."

And that was it. He let me escape to my room, where I had all the time I needed to get back to my schoolwork. Not that I could concentrate much at that point. Was it really so simple? A shake of the head, and no awkward words?

I should have been relieved. For some reason, though, I felt oddly bereft. The evening seemed wrong without its usual punctuation of question and refusal. What was I supposed to do now?

Be careful what you wish for, some part of my mind jeered at me, and I told it to shut up, and then went to my computer to check my messages.

Despite these small bumps, and despite a growing sense of unease that I had made some sort of fatal mistake, the pace of our lives continued without much disruption. It was something of a shock when I received my final grades several weeks later and realized I had been living under Sarzhin's roof for almost three months.

I had a month-long break before my next round of classes started, and I didn't quite know what I would do with myself. True, I could increase my time with Sarzhin in the greenhouse, but I worried being around him that much more would only contribute to the awkwardness between us. I had been using my schoolwork as something of a buffer, a welcome distraction to keep me occupied. Sarzhin had accepted my course load without question, but now I was unencumbered, I worried what he might think if I kept coming up with excuses to stay away from him.

Not that I disliked being in his presence. Nothing so simple as that. When we put aside our uneasy detente, I did like talking to him. For all his isolation here, he was extremely well-read and appeared quite interested in interplanetary politics. He provided insights that I know helped me with some of my papers, especially the ones on xenolinguistics. If circumstances had been different, he was actually someone whose company I might have sought, just because I enjoyed being around him more than I did just about anyone else on Lathvin, with the possible exception of my father. In fact, loath as I still was to admit it to myself, I had actually become quite fond of the Zhore.

Fondness, however, isn't too sturdy a basis for a marriage.

My father and I had continued to exchange messages on a daily basis, and from time to time I'd even get one from my mother. Not that she ever said anything much beyond hoping that I was well. As dull as her mail might be, at least I didn't have to continually dodge questions from her the way I did with my father. I'm sure he knew I was hiding something, but I kept my word to Sarzhin—I said nothing of the marriage proposals, even though they appeared to have stopped for the moment.

One morning, only a few days into my break from university, I received mail from my father with astonishing news: Libba was engaged, to a junior professor at Epsilon Eridani. Even more amazing, she was traveling with her fiancé to Lathvin IV so he could meet the family, and my father wanted to know if I could possibly come to visit for a few days?

I wanted to say yes, but of course I had no idea how Sarzhin would respond to such a request. Still, as Libba and Cole were apparently already en route, I knew I'd have to ask sooner than later.

At that time of day I knew I'd most likely find the Zhore out the greenhouse, waiting for me to join him, as we generally did most of our work in the morning, sometimes continuing into the afternoon if the project was involved enough. Sure enough, he was there tending a row of carnivorous orchids from Cygnus Alpha. Luckily, we were both far too large to be considered prey by the orchids; their preferred snacks were small insects. At least I'd timed my arrival well, as the flowers were all shuddering by the time I got there, the sign that they'd already been fed and were happily digesting their late-morning meal.

Sarzhin turned as I approached. "What is it, Anika?"

"I just had mail from my father."

"And?"

Why did it suddenly feel so difficult to make such a simple request? "My sister is coming for a visit—with her fiancé. So my parents would very much appreciate it if you would let me go see her."

He said nothing at first, but only set down the plastic container and pair of long-nosed tweezers he'd been holding…the delivery method for feeding the orchids, which did have a tendency to nip. When he spoke at last, his voice sounded oddly strained. "For how long?"

I lifted my shoulders. "I'm not sure. A week or so. She's supposed to arrive the day after tomorrow."

"I can't let you go for that long."

The comment was delivered in such a matter-of-fact way that it took me a few seconds to fully digest it. "You can't—why not? I've been here for over three months, and you won't let me go for even a week?"

"A week is...impossible." He turned toward me, gloved hands knotted into the folds of his robe.

"Impossible?" I repeated. Anger flared in me then, for his flat refusal, for the hours and minutes he'd taken of my own life with no apologies, no explanations. It wasn't as if I'd announced that I was leaving, never to return. I didn't bother to moderate my tone as I continued, "You want to know what's impossible? Forcing someone to come live with you for no reason, resorting to blackmail, asking—" And I broke off then, because somehow I knew bringing up the marriage proposals was a line I didn't want to cross.

He held up a hand. "Enough, Anika. I did not say you could not go. I only said you could not go for a full week."

"Why not?"

"It is not enough that I said it was impossible?"

"Not if you won't tell me why."

"I cannot do that."

I crossed my arms and glared at him. By that time I had already begun to be quite tired of the mysteries and the unanswered questions. His refusal to grant what seemed to me a very simple request only infuriated me that much more.

He took a step toward me and then paused. Somehow I knew he wanted to reach out to me, but had stopped himself at the last minute. "You will see your family," he said quietly. "For three days. On the morning of the third day, you must return here to me."

"And if I don't?"

"If you don't—well, let us just say the outcome will be something neither one of us desires."

Which I guessed was code for him reporting my father to the magistrate, although one would think there had to be some sort of statute of limitations on petty thefts such as my father's appropriation of Sarzhin's moonflowers.

Three days. I had no idea how I could explain myself to my parents, or worse, Libba and her fiancé, but I supposed I could come up with something. My father's message had said the pair planned to remain on Lathvin for some two weeks; any shorter a stay, and the trip here wouldn't have been worth the effort. Three days seemed like a pitifully short time, considering that I hadn't seen my sister in more than five years. Still, it was better than nothing.

"Fine," I said. "If you want to be unreasonable, I guess there isn't much I can do about it. I'll let my father know I'll be there two days from now. That'll give Libba and her fiancé time to arrive on-planet and get settled in."

Sarzhin replied, "I am sorry you think I am being unreasonable. If you only knew—"

"Yes, if I only knew," I cut in. "Unfortunately, as you don't seem inclined to tell me anything, it's sort of hard for me to know what the hell you're talking about!"

With that I stormed out of the greenhouse, a little astonished at myself for confronting him in such a way.

He made no move to stop me, but only watched in silence as I left. And later that evening as we sat down to dinner, he said nothing of our earlier scene.

Perhaps it was spiteful of me, but that night I almost wished he would ask me to marry him again, just so I would have the opportunity to turn him down.

Although Sarzhin might have been parsimonious in the time he had allotted me to visit my family, otherwise he took every care to ensure I would go there and come back safely. My family's homestead lay a little more than five kilometers away from his property, a distance I could have easily walked, even in the constant rainstorms that plagued the planet, but he insisted I take the spare transport vehicle after he learned I could drive one well enough.

"That way, you can get home more quickly," he told me, after he handed me the vehicle's remote.

Which home? I wondered. *Yours...or my parents'?*

Really, I didn't even know which place I could call home. I had spent every waking moment of the last three months in Sarzhin's house, but it still didn't feel quite mine. I had been a given place to stay in it, no more. However, the thought of the homestead where I had grown to adulthood seemed curiously remote, like something I once read about in a story but could no longer recall with any distinctness.

My things had already been packed in the small

satchel I'd brought from home; no need for a bigger case when I only needed to take with me clothing for three days. The garage was located on the east side of the mansion and housed both transports, along with piles of equipment and machinery, only some of which I was able to identify. Ever since he'd told me of the spare vehicle, I'd wondered why he needed two of them when he lived here alone. I knew better than to ask, however.

"By noon of the third day," he told me. "No later."

"I know," I said. Really, did he think I could possibly forget that? If I didn't return on time, would he use the other transport to come and get me? Somehow I doubted it, although I did almost smile at the thought of Sarzhin showing up on my parents' doorstep to fetch me back like some sort of black-robed truant officer.

"Go, then. You can reach me by comm if necessary." He paused and added, "Enjoy your time with your family."

"I will." Since there didn't seem to be much else for me to do, I gave him an awkward little wave, and climbed up into the transport and closed the door behind me. The familiar whistling sound of the cabin pressurizing surrounded me. Of course I carried my breather on the passenger seat, just in case—no inhabitant of Lathvin went anywhere without the apparatus within arm's length—but the transport was, unlike the one my father had crashed, new and in good repair.

I waited until I saw Sarzhin go out the airlock door that connected the house to the garage, and then pressed the remote to open the pressure door to the outside. At

once a blast of wind and rain swept in. With a sigh, I acti-
vated the windshield wipers and hoped Libba's fiancé was
an indoor person. There wasn't much in the way of outdoor recreation on Lathvin IV, that was for sure.

A smoothly paved drive connected the garage to the
road and cut through one of the fields of moonflowers that
surrounded Sarzhin's house. The road itself wasn't in nearly
as good repair, but the all-terrain treads on the transport
didn't seem to care one way or another, and I moved along
at a decent clip. Almost before I knew it, I had reached the
turnoff for the homestead, and I pointed the vehicle down
a drive that seemed far narrower than it had only a few
months ago. Through the driving rain I saw another transport parked off to one side of the house. I didn't recognize
it but guessed it was the replacement for the one my father
had crashed. It actually looked newish and bigger than the
old one, and I wondered how my father had been able to
wrangle enough replacement funds out of the insurance
company to get something so nice.

I supposed I would learn soon enough. Slowing to
a crawl, I eased Sarzhin's transport into the space next to
the other vehicle, and then picked up the breather and
set it over my mouth and nose. I stowed the remote in my
pocket and secured the rain flaps of my poncho around
my neck. Not that it really mattered—somehow Lathvin's
freezing, needle-sharp raindrops always managed to find
their way inside any protective garment you put on.

Satchel in one hand, I opened the door with my other
hand and slid out, gasping a little as the cold, thin air hit

my face. I realized that I hadn't actually been outside since I had arrived in the Zhore's home. I also realized I hadn't missed the fresh air one bit—the interior of the greenhouse had far "fresher" air, when you got right down to it, considering all the plants exhaling in that one spot.

Head bent down, I hurried over to the airlock and hit the button. The door slid upward and I stepped inside, then did the customary shake to get as much moisture off me as possible. Airlocks never had security locks on them—you never knew when someone might need some last-minute shelter from the planet's unbreathable air. The actual lock was on the door that separated the interior of the house from the airlock, but of course even a place as modest as my family's homestead had an intercom.

I pressed the "talk" switch. "Hey, it's me—I mean, it's Anika. Somebody open the door—I'm freezing out here."

Almost at once the door into the house opened, and I emerged into a hubbub of voices and exclamations. I saw my father and mother first, and then Libba, who somehow looked much more grown-up in person, even though I'd seen vids of her just three months ago. Just behind her was a tall, fair-haired young man I didn't recognize but knew had to be her fiancé. No purple skin or antennas. Not that I'd really expected her to get engaged to an Eridani; she was too conventional for that, and besides, the planet had a sizable Gaian expat community because of the universities that dotted its surface.

After the quiet elegance of Sarzhin's home, the overall effect of all those voices at once was a little overwhelming.

I blinked, and managed a smile, even as my father came forward and said, "Let's get that poncho before it drips on everything."

I reached up to undo the rain flaps and the fasteners of my damp outer garment and lifted it away. Even from across the room I could see Libba's eyebrows shoot up. The wine-colored tunic and pants I wore were just as elegant as her own off-world outfit. I guessed she hadn't been expecting that.

Then came the introductions—Libba's fiancé was named Cole Mikkels, and he was a junior professor of astrophysics, which I had to admit sounded terribly impressive. They had met at the university, but not because she'd been in any of his classes. No, she'd been earning some money on the side by tending bar at school functions, and they'd struck up a conversation at the astrophysics department's mixer. If someone had asked me, I would have told them my sister didn't know the difference between a martini and a Centauri pile driver, but obviously she'd been learning a bit more during the past five years than differential equations and Stacian declensions.

"But you," she said, running a practiced gaze over my elegant ensemble, "you look quite different, Anika. Dad told me you were actually staying with that Zhore down the road. What's going on with that?"

I shot a glare at my father, who gave a little shrug, as if to say, *I had to tell her something to explain where you were.*

"Yes," I said, trying to ignore my mother's look of

sharpened interest, "he's…well, he's an expert botanist, and I'm sort of studying with him in addition to my university coursework. Kind of an apprenticeship, I guess." That seemed the best explanation, since Sarzhin really was an expert, and I'd learned enough from working with him over the past few weeks that I thought I could do a reasonably good job of faking it if someone really wanted to start asking questions about what I'd learned so far.

Libba's eyebrows got another workout. "I didn't know you were that into botany."

"Oh, yes. It's really fascinating. And Sar—that is, the Zhore says it's a good field to go into. You know, he sold one of his Azar lilies to the CEO of the Gaian Relocation Corporation for ten thousand units."

At that remark everyone started talking at once, asking me about what other sorts of plants he raised, and how much they sold for, and saying it was no wonder he had gotten such nice clothes for me. That is, my mother and father and Libba were the ones peppering me with questions and comments, and Cole sort of stood off to one wide and watched the commotion. I deflected the questions as best I could and gave them the few bits of information I deemed safe.

Finally things calmed down enough for my mother to say she needed to get back into the kitchen, and would Anika lend her a hand?

I went without protest, mostly because I'd always been the one to help my mother out with the cooking. Libba had never been very domestic. Also, my mother was less likely to continue the inquisition.

The hope that she wouldn't ask any more questions died, however, after she handed me a spoon and instructed me to stir the contents of the pot, which looked like her famous goulash. I couldn't remember the last time she'd made it, though. Obviously she was breaking out the big guns for Cole, the junior professor of astrophysics.

"I suppose he has you help out with the cooking."

"He who?" I asked innocently.

"You know very well who. The Zhore."

I shook my head and inhaled the wonderful paprika-laced steam that rose from the pot. "No, I've never even been in the kitchen. He has a mech for that."

She turned away from the tomatoes she was slicing. From the looks of it, my parents had donated the bulk of their current hydroponic crop for this one meal. "A mech?"

"Yes," I replied, feeling somehow uneasy, although I couldn't really say why. "The mech takes care of all the household stuff."

"So he really is rich."

"I guess so."

"We thought so, after he sent the transport, but—"

"What transport?"

"Why, the one sitting outside. Surely you saw it. You didn't think your father and I could have afforded that, did you?"

No, I hadn't, but I also hadn't thought Sarzhin would be the reason why they had such a fine replacement vehicle. My tone flat, I said, "Dad never told me anything about that."

"Of course he didn't. The Zhore specifically said we weren't supposed to say anything to you. At least, that's what your father explained to me."

Now, why Sarzhin didn't see fit to tell me he had paid for my parents' replacement transport, I had no idea. I also didn't know why he'd done it in the first place. It wasn't his fault my father had lost control in that freakish storm and wrecked the thing. Did the Zhore feel some sort of remorse for blackmailing me away from my family? That didn't make any sense, though. He could have sent me home at any time if he were really racked with guilt over the whole thing, but that sure hadn't happened.

I shrugged and said as noncommittally as I could, "That was nice of him."

"Indeed it was." She set down the knife and began sprinkling greenhouse basil over the tops of the tomatoes. "It seems he's taking good care of you—and us. Has he never said why he wanted you there?"

"No, never," I lied. Maybe the Zhores disliked dishonesty, but it was common currency for the human race, and besides, I'd promised Sarzhin I wouldn't tell the truth about my situation to my family. I wasn't about to start poking at my reasons for why I considered my loyalty to Sarzhin to be more important than loyalty to my family.

"Hmm." Apparently finished with the basil, she put it back in its self-sealing container and returned it to the food storage unit. Then she cocked her head to one side and said in musing tones, "He is very rich, though."

"I—I suppose so."

"Is he old?"

"What?" I turned away from the goulash and frowned at her. "What has that got to do with anything?"

She echoed my shrug of a minute earlier. Who knows—I could have picked up the gesture from her, even though I tended to favor my father in terms of coloring and facial features. "It's just that, if he's elderly, maybe he wants someone to, I don't know, be his heir."

Her casual greed surprised me more than I really wanted to admit. No wonder she hadn't communicated much with me, or asked much about Sarzhin. In her mind she'd probably already been calculating how much I stood to inherit from the alien who had taken me in.

I said, "No, he's not old. At least, he doesn't act or sound like he's elderly."

Not that that meant much, when it came to aliens. The humanoid race from Tau Ceti had the astonishing ability to appear in the prime of life right up until the minute they dropped dead. Nice trick, I always thought. But I remembered the strength of Sarzhin's hands as they had held mine, and the muscles in his arm when I had laid my hand there. Nothing about him spoke of age or infirmity.

"Oh," she replied, without making any effort to hide the disappointment in her voice. "But he is teaching you something about botany, right?"

"Yes," I said. I knew she needed to pin her hopes on something for me, as there didn't seem to be much chance of me getting off-world the way Libba had. "He's teaching me a great deal."

Dinner wasn't quite as awkward as I thought it would be, since Libba and Cole carried a good deal of the conversation by recounting more stories about their life at the university and their circle of friends. As I listened to them talk, I almost felt as if I had somehow become alien myself, my life with Sarzhin so very different from what she described. Even if I had stayed at home, we had very little social activity here on Lathvin to speak of. The homesteads were spread just far enough apart so the sort of casual socializing that went on in more heavily populated worlds didn't really occur here. True, Port Natchez was something of a gathering place, but the pub there wasn't exactly the sort of venue my parents would have wanted me to frequent, and beyond that the little spaceport town didn't have much to offer.

It turned out the engaged couple was staying in the small bedroom Libba and I had once shared, and so I ended up on the couch. I didn't bother to protest. They were the guests of honor, not I, and I supposed I could put up with the lumpy old sofa for a few days, even though I couldn't help contrasting it with my luxurious bed back at Sarzhin's home.

That first night it took me a long time to fall asleep. The bumpy couch had something to do with it, I knew, and maybe it was also that the sound of the weather seemed so much more omnipresent here than it was in Sarzhin's house. There, the thick walls and triple-sealed windows shut out all but the faintest whisper of the rain-drops, while here it sounded as if I had the entire percussion session of the Gaian Grand Philharmonic beating on the roof directly over my head. And behind that was the convulsive chugging of the atmospheric generator, adding its dull thumps to the cacophony.

Still, eventually I did fall asleep, and was chased in and out of slumber by a series of disquieting dreams whose content I forgot almost as soon as I opened my eyes to the darkness.

Except one.

It seemed I was back in the house I shared with Sarzhin, but it was only a shell of the graceful home I remembered. The windows were all gone, the elegant wall fountains and their attendant greenery dry and bar-ren. A cold wind whistled through the empty rooms. Even in my dream I knew I shouldn't have been able to breathe, not with the building unsealed and Lathvin's unbreathable air flowing all around me, but somehow I was able to keep walking, arms wrapped around me to keep out the chill.

I saw no sign of Sarzhin, not in the library, or the din-ing room, or even the greenhouse, which was filled with the husks of dead plants, the leaves and flowers he had once so lovingly tended now brittle and brown, shriveled from their exposure to the planet's unforgiving atmosphere. My dream-self wanted to weep at the loss of all those beautiful plants. Somehow, though, I kept walking, my feet taking me up the stairs to the one section of the house where I had never been…Sarzhin's room.

The door stood open, and I hesitated on the threshold, even in the dream nervous about crossing over into such interdicted territory. A cold wind blew through the open windows here as well, and inside everything was bare. No furniture, no bed, nothing but an expanse of dark, polished stone floor, and some shredded curtains of heavy black fabric fluttering at the window.

Only they weren't fabric. They moved, and came toward me, and even as I opened my mouth to cry out, I heard Sarzhin's voice say my name, and the great folds of his cloak flowed around me, pulling me into his warmth. His arms were around me, and I pressed myself to him, sobbing at last, clinging to him with desperate fingers. And then all around was light and the green of growing things, as the house seemed to heal itself the longer we held each other, until at last we sank down on the floor, mouths touching, hands reaching…reaching…

I sat up in bed with a gasp, and the familiar, faintly goulash-scented confines of my family's living room met my straining eyes. Save for the incessant pounding of the rain overhead, all was quiet. No one seemed to have been disturbed by the nightmare.

No one except me, of course.

Shivering, I pulled the covers up to my chin and tried to will away the lingering sensations from the dream—the feel of his body against mine, the touch of his mouth. It had felt awfully human.

Because it was a dream, I told myself. A crazy, stupid dream…brought on, I guessed, by the over-spiced goulash. Even now my stomach rumbled a bit, unsure as to how it should handle such a dish after months of eating the more subtly seasoned Zhore food. Yes, that had to be it.

Even so, I found myself reluctant to go back to sleep. I tossed and turned, and after a few more minutes fished my tablet out of my satchel and brought up a silly adventure vid I'd probably watched a dozen times already, about the adventures of a ship's crew just on this side of the law, with a new twist or turn every few minutes. Usually it would have amused me. This time, though, I found it almost impossible to concentrate, my brain still buzzing with the sensations from my dream. Never mind that they weren't real. They had felt real.

Too real.

No one seemed to notice I was bleary-eyed and cranky the next morning. My parents probably attributed it to the fact that we had to queue for the shower, as the homestead had only the one bathroom, and so I had to wait almost two hours before I could get ready in the morning. By the time I finally did get in there, the dream had begun to fade, and I forced myself to think of other things, to convince myself that these little inconveniences were nothing, and that I should be glad to be seeing my family again. If only the house didn't feel as if it were about to burst at the seams with five adults crammed into it.

What Cole and Libba could possibly find to do to occupy themselves for a full two weeks here, I had no idea, but it turned out Libba wanted to go over some of the wedding plans with my mother, and the two of them spent a good deal of time on the computer comparing designs and menus. I supposed Cole was going to pay for all of it—fare off-world included—as I knew my parents could never afford such an expense.

It seemed she'd already chosen some friends from the university as her attendants, a fact for which I was grateful. She made an off-hand apology, saying it was just more convenient to have them in the wedding party than a sister who lived light-years away, and of course I told her that was fine. And it was; if Sarzhin would only let me leave his home for three days at a time, I was sure there was no way he would allow me to travel all the way to Epsilon Eridani, a trip of several days even on the fastest subspace-drive ships. No doubt a battle would ensue once my family found out I couldn't leave Lathvin to attend the wedding, but that was still some standard months off, and I figured I'd worry about it when the time came.

Later that morning, Libba, Cole, and my mother headed into Port Natchez to do some shopping at the commissary. They tried to get me to go as well, but dealing with even the three of them was proving to be more work than I expected. I knew I didn't want to go to the commissary and be surrounded by yet more people. Besides, I didn't really know what my parents had been saying about my absence, but if the Port Natchez regulars had heard anything about me living with Sarzhin, then I guessed I'd be peppered with even more questions. So I demurred, saying I wanted to help my father in the greenhouse. No one seemed inclined to argue with that. I think they were all hoping I'd impart some of my secret Zhore-obtained gardening knowledge.

Compared to the enormous structure at the back of Sarzhin's home, the little setup my parents had seemed pitifully small. But the warm, humid air was familiar, as well as the scent of green, growing things. My father and I puttered a bit in companionable silence. He was probably glad of the chance for some peace and quiet as well.

Then I said, "Mom told me about the transport."

He set down the delicate shears he'd been holding and picked up a misting bottle. "She did, did she?"

"Yes. It sounds like she's hoping Sar—the Zhore will drop dead and leave me all his money."

"Oh, good lord." With his free hand he poked in the soil substitute at the base of a tomato plant. "She doesn't mean any harm, you know."

"I guess."

During this exchange he had kept his attention focused on the plant, but now he straightened and set the misting bottle aside and gazed at me frankly. It was odd to be looking at a human face other than my own after so much time—his face was familiar, every line and feature immediately recognizable, from his graying dark hair to his blue eyes and square chin, and yet at the same time something felt off, as if I had expected him to somehow look different.

"I didn't tell you about the transport because I was specifically told not to. Odd fellow, that Zhore of yours."

"He's not my Zhore."

"Figure of speech. Anyway, I noticed you didn't say much about him."

"There isn't a lot to say."

The look he sent in my direction following that remark was frankly disbelieving.

"No, really," I protested. "I mean, he's made sure I'm more than comfortable—my bedroom is almost as big as this house—and if I need something for my coursework he gets it for me, but it's not as if we're hosting fabulous parties over there or something. We live a very quiet life."

"We," my father repeated in significant tones.

"Well, it is just the two of us, unless you count the mech." Which you really couldn't, since mechs didn't exactly have personalities. They just did what they were told, in an unobtrusive way I guessed a human servant could never match. "But the Zhore works in his greenhouse, and I mostly stay in my room and do schoolwork, except for the times I go help him with the plants or whatever. It's really pretty dull."

"All right…if you say so." He picked up his shears and moved on to the next tomato plant. "So what do you think of all this wedding commotion?"

"Libba seems happy," I replied cautiously. I wasn't quite sure what he expected me to say.

"Oh, yes. She's done very well for herself, our Libba." His expression sobered, and he added, "I've often wondered if we really did the right thing by coming here."

I'd wondered the same thing myself over the past few years, but I doubted that was what he wanted to hear. I said, "Dad, it's been fine—"

"Has it?" He shook his head. "The GRC sold us a bill of goods, and I think both you and I know that. Sure, Libba's fine, but the only reason she's fine is because she got off-world. But what about you, Anika?"

"What about me?"

"I know you were disappointed that you couldn't go away to school. And now, this arrangement with the Zhore—" A wave of anger passed over his face, and he abruptly tossed the pruning shears onto the gardening cart that stood a few paces off. "I should never have agreed to that."

Trying to sound calm and reasonable, I said, "What else were you supposed to do? And it's not that I mind. Really."

I had intended only to reassure him, but I realized as I spoke that I meant what I said. Something in the quiet life I had been leading appealed to me in ways I hadn't even considered until I had a chance to step back and think about them from a distance. I liked having enough time to study and do my work properly, and not sandwich it in between all the chores I'd had at the homestead. I liked learning about the plants and flowers Sarzhin raised. I liked the meals we shared and the discussions we had. In short, I liked him.

My father sent another of those skeptical glances my way. "You don't mind living there."

"No." I hesitated, then said, "We get along pretty well. In the time I've been there, I've—well, I guess you could say I've become rather fond of him." As soon as the words left my mouth, I realized I'd probably made a mistake.

My father frowned. "Fond?" He sounded as if he had never heard the word before. A warning note entered his voice. "Anika—"

"Oh, Dad, don't turn nothing into something. I am fond of him—he's smart and polite and well-read. He treats me with respect. That's it."

For a few seconds my father didn't say anything, but just watched me carefully. "You've never said why he wanted you there."

"That's because he's never told me. Maybe he just wants the company. The mech isn't a great conversationalist, after all."

"Maybe," my father remarked, but he didn't sound convinced.

I held my breath, waiting for the follow-up question.

It never came. My father retrieved the misting bottle and moved down the row of plants, then stopped at one and bent over a leaf. "Could you take a look at this squash? I've never seen brown spots like this before."

And I went over to inspect the plant in question, relieved he'd apparently decided to let the matter go. I didn't like having to lie to him.

Maybe it was because I had just begun to understand that I was lying to myself as well.

The following day the whole lot of us went to see the Mirsalis Caves, which were Lathvin IV's one interesting geological feature. I couldn't extricate myself from this outing without appearing completely antisocial, so I went along with as good grace as I could muster, although spending two hours squeezed in the back of the transport as we bumped along poorly maintained roads was not exactly my idea of a fun time. I hadn't seen the caves since I was twelve, though, and therefore I told myself the expedition wasn't a complete waste of time.

It was clear that my parents were trying to do everything they could to keep Cole entertained during his time here on Lathvin. What they planned after this, having already exhausted the commissary in Port Natchez, I couldn't guess. However, I supposed it wasn't my problem, since I was going to be leaving the next morning anyway. That little tidbit hadn't gone over very well with my parents or my sister, but I'd stood firm and told them it was impossible for me to stay any longer than that.

The caves were beautiful, though, their walls encrusted with minerals that refracted light every which way, pale stalactites reflecting in pools of black water that had never seen the sun. Even having a bunch of tourists tromping around in the caves couldn't quite break their spell.

I did notice Cole didn't appear quite as enchanted as the rest of us, and once or twice I was pretty sure I saw an expression of boredom flit across his features. Well, compared to the rarefied and intellectual atmosphere of the university on Eridani, I supposed this was all pretty tame stuff. Most likely he was just enduring this trip for Libba's sake and couldn't wait to get away from her bumpkin family and Lathvin in general. Truth be told, this was an inconsequential backwater planet, one that might be useful in another fifty years once the atmospheric generators had done their job but in the meantime wasn't worth much. I couldn't even find it in me to dislike Cole for his disinterest. It wasn't as if I thought Lathvin was so great, either. And he had come all this way, which meant he had to care about my sister enough to do that much.

He did stay close to her, and several times I saw him reach out to steady her by the elbow when the footing in certain parts of the cave got a little treacherous. As I watched them together, I couldn't help wondering what it would be like to share that closeness with someone. And for some reason I recalled the feel of Sarzhin's hands as they had closed around mine, the strength of his arm beneath my fingertips. How his arms had gone around me in my dream.

That was just crazy, though, and I gave myself a little mental shake as I followed my parents up and out of the caves. We'd been wearing breathers the whole time, as the cost of sealing off the caves to keep a breathable atmosphere inside would have been prohibitive. However, there was a small restaurant and souvenir shop near the caves, where we all stopped to get some lunch, and of course we were able to remove the breathers once we were safely inside.

I was quiet as we all took a table off in one corner, thoughts still occupied by those unwanted remembrances of Sarzhin's touch. At least, I told myself they were unwanted. Probably I was just feeling isolated and something like a fifth wheel, and Sarzhin was the only real companion I had at the moment. I supposed it was only natural I'd be thinking of him. Who else would I think of? Eli Barleigh, who was the mechanic's assistant in Port Natchez's one and only transport repair shop, and who'd drunk too much of that nasty retsina the night of Libba's going-away party and decided it was his chance to back me into a corner and steal a kiss? Not likely. Even now the memory was enough to make me shudder.

My mother and Libba began to discuss more wedding details, and I tuned them out, instead looking up to read the menu offerings on the electronic board on the wall next to us.

But then I heard my sister say, "Of course Anika will come," and I blinked, focusing on her for the first time since we'd sat down.

"Come where?" I asked.

"We're going to take a little expedition up to the

duty-free center on Four-A tomorrow."

"Four-A" was slang for the larger of Lathvin's two moons, the one with the spaceport. "I can't go shopping with you tomorrow," I said flatly. "I have to head back to Sar—I have to head back. I can't be any later than noon."

Libba scowled at me. "Don't be silly. It's just a hop and a jump. We'll take the early shuttle. You'll be back by thirteen hundred at the latest."

"Which is already too late," I told her. "Since I just said I had to be back at the Zhore's house by noon."

My sister sent a pleading look in our mother's direction. "But I wanted to buy her an outfit for the wedding. I'm trying to do something nice."

"Anika, what difference could one hour possibly make?"

With them massed like that against me, I knew I didn't have much of a chance. If I begged off, then I was just being ungrateful, since Libba was ostensibly doing me a favor by buying me something I could wear to her wedding. That she probably had decided to do me this "favor" simply so I wouldn't embarrass her by showing up in something unsuitable didn't really enter the equation. And if I said I wouldn't even be attending the wedding because there was no way I could leave Sarzhin for that long, then I'd be opening a can of Centauri ink worms, and I really didn't want to fight that particular battle right then.

"I don't know," I replied. I knew I sounded as sulky as a thirteen-year-old caught skimping on her chores, but at the moment I didn't care. "I guess it'll be all right—as long as we take the early shuttle."

"Not a problem," Libba said promptly. "I'd already planned on it, just to accommodate you."

Right, I thought, but I decided silence was probably the wiser course. I nodded and even forced out a smile, but something inside me knotted—and it wasn't because of hunger pangs. I didn't want to contemplate how angry Sarzhin might be if I were late returning home.

True to her word, my sister was ready very early the next morning, early enough that we could catch the eight hundred shuttle from Port Natchez. I was feeling less than sanguine about the success of the day, but it seemed so far everything was going according to plan. We took the first shuttle and were up at the Four-A spaceport in less than half an hour.

The stores there operated around the clock, as of course incoming and outgoing long-distance flights didn't bother to adhere to local time. We tromped around the duty-free area as Libba had me try on various outfits and then ended up rejecting them one by one. The whole procedure only served to make me increasingly irritated, as I knew she was just wasting my time—even if she didn't realize it yet. Besides, I had clothing back at Sarzhin's house as nice as the pieces she was selecting, but whenever I tried to point that out, she responded in typical fashion by either rolling her eyes or ignoring me.

Of course my mother was no help. She just would say, "Do this for your sister," or "What difference could one more outfit make?" In the grand scheme of things, maybe not that much, but by the time we walked into the fifth store I was ready to scream. Really, how many shops could a spaceport in such a backwater system support?

In fact, I did let out a little shriek when I stepped out of the dressing room in the last store, only to see that the chronograph on the wall opposite read 11:55.

"The shuttle's leaving in five minutes!"

Libba sent a languid glance over her shoulder at the chronograph. "Oh, foo. That's nothing. Besides, they never leave on time."

"How would you know?" I retorted, and immediately retreated to reclaim my own clothes so we could get the hell out of there. This procedure only took a minute, and I bolted for the door even as I finished shaking my hair free of my tunic's collar.

"Don't you think you're being a little dramatic?" Libba demanded, as she and my mother started trotting after me.

Of course the final store just had to be located on almost the opposite end of the facility and two levels down from the shuttle pad. Somehow I managed to keep from running, but I did speed-walk the entire length of the spaceport and then burst into the disembarkation area — only to see the gates closed and the sleek shape of the planet-hopper blasting up into the black sky.

I let out an incoherent sound of dismay and ran to the window, a huge expanse of vacuum-rated clear polymer.

There I paused, hands pressed flat against the cool plastic, as if somehow I could force myself through it and on into one of the seats of the disappearing shuttle.

"Oops," said Libba, and I rounded on her.

"This is all your fault!"

Her green eyes widened. "Oh, please, Anika, can you spare me the Greek tragedy? It's just a missed shuttle—the next one will be along in…" She paused and looked up at the board above the ticketing desk. "Four hours."

"Four hours!" I wailed, and then ran for the comm station at the far side of the waiting area.

But when I typed in Sarzhin's comm code, I got only a hiss of dead air. My hand shaking, I tried again. Nothing.

Ignoring my mother and sister, who looked at me as if I'd just lost my mind, I practically ran over to the ticketing counter. "Excuse me."

The clerk there didn't even look up from his computer screen. "Mmm?"

"Your comms don't seem to be working."

He gave a laconic shrug. "Solar storms. Been playing havoc with our systems the past two standard. It's a mess getting signals down to the planet. You'd have better luck direct-dialing Eridani. Heh."

I didn't find anything remotely funny in the situation. All I could do was turn away from him and stare out the windows in the waiting area. I couldn't even see the shuttle anymore.

My mother shook her head at me. "Goodness, Anika,

you're acting like your best friend just died. You can just explain to the Zhore that you missed the shuttle and the comms were down. It's certainly not the end of the world."

I stared at her, at my sister, seeing in their blank, mystified faces absolutely no comprehension or sympathy. How could I explain to them that I had promised Sarzhin I would return on time, and how betraying that promise now seemed like the worst thing I could possibly have done to him? They would never understand. I hardly understood myself.

"No, it's not the end of the world," I told her in curt tones I would never have used on my mother a few months ago. I turned away from her to stare at the black heavens outside. "At least, I hope it isn't."

The joy definitely went out of the shopping trip after that, and even when my sister offered to buy lunch at one of the spaceport's cafés I barely ate anything, but only took a few token sips of my soup while she and my mother snacked on soufflés and sparkling water. They appeared to dismiss my black mood as an outrageous case of the sulks and mostly ignored me from there on out as they discussed menus and color schemes and the sorts of flowers available on Eridani. At least my sister knew better than to ask me to try on any more clothes. I did follow them grimly as they went back to a few of the shops where I had had no luck but Libba had seen something she liked, and she did end up purchasing a few outfits — all on Cole's tab, I was certain. Somehow I managed to hold my tongue and not ask her whether she'd be over her weight allowance for the return trip if she kept adding new clothes.

Finally it was time to catch the sixteen hundred shuttle. I insisted on being in the debarkation area a good half-hour before the shuttle's departure, and at least my mother and sister had the good sense not to argue with me. On the trip back I said nothing, but only stared out one of the viewports as the bruise-colored disk of Lathvin grew larger and larger, and we eventually descended through the soupy gray clouds.

At least I had had the presence of mind to pack everything before we left for Four-A, so once we returned to the homestead all I had to do was gather up my satchel and leave. I gave my father a quick hug, told a rather startled-looking Cole that it had been very nice to meet him, and then put on my breather and bolted for the airlock.

By then it was almost seventeen hundred, and Lathvin's quick-falling dusk was upon me. I climbed into the transport, turned on the headlights, and headed toward Sarzhin's property, pressing down on the accelerator with a reckless disregard for the pouring rain and the increasing darkness. In fact, I was going so fast I almost missed the turnoff, but at the last minute I saw the small break in the ranks of moonflowers where the drive was located and took a hard left. The treads snarled at me a little bit, but the traction held, and soon enough I was approaching the garage.

I pushed the button on the remote and pulled inside, then shut the door again so the garage compartment could repressurize. I knew it was silly to expect Sarzhin to be waiting for me here, but even so I couldn't help looking around as I got out of the vehicle. No one was there, of course.

After grabbing my satchel, I headed for the door into the house. It was quiet and dim in there, all the hall sconces burning at quarter-power, which was unusual for the time of day. Usually they were only set at that level during the overnight hours.

"Sarzhin?" I called out, but only silence met my straining ears.

Hmm. I placed my satchel on the bottom step of the staircase and drew off my rain poncho as well. I could have gone up to my room, but I wanted to see him, and I doubted he would be on that level, as his study and the library and the other rooms he utilized the most were located on the ground floor.

He was in neither of those places. The dark images from my dream of two nights earlier rose in my mind, of the house abandoned and dead. I told myself not to be an idiot, that of course Sarzhin must be out back, tending to his plants. I bolted into the greenhouse at a half-run, but then pulled up short as the air seemed to suddenly be ripped from my lungs. Gasping, I paused and looked around, only to see that many of the plants were drooping, dying in their carefully arranged rows. A faint whistling sound reached my ears.

I shut my eyes and told myself not to panic, that surely there must be a logical explanation for all this.

Emergency breathers hung from a rack next to the door. It was extremely unlikely that the sturdy polymer out of which the greenhouse had been constructed would ever rip, but Sarzhin was not the type to take chances. I grasped one of the breathers and fastened it over my face, and then took a second breathing apparatus and tucked it into my belt before I headed toward the very rear of the greenhouse, where I knew a secondary door and airlock were located.

Both were open, subjecting the greenhouse and all the tender plants inside it to the painfully thin atmosphere. I closed them behind me as I went outside and prayed I hadn't been too late to keep them all from dying of exposure.

The tall stalks of the moonflowers crowded around me, seeming to glow in the growing darkness. Between them I could see a faint path, as if someone had stumbled or fought his way through the crowding plants. I followed the path, my own breathing harsh in my ears, my heart beating painfully in my chest. The cold rain soaked my clothing at once, but I hardly noticed the chill. On Lathvin, it wasn't the cold or the damp that killed you.

I found him lying in a messy black heap some hundred yards from the house. The cloak and hood still shrouded him. Pale moonflowers bent over him, ethereal mourners.

"Sarzhin!" I cried, and knelt next to him in the mud.

Grasping him by the shoulders, I turned him over onto his back. The sodden hood draped itself across his face. I had no idea how long he had been out here, but somehow that didn't matter. I knew I must try to save him, even if he had been lying in the mud for hours.

One moonflower nodded particularly close, and I grabbed it and pressed it against his still-hidden visage. I saw no stir, no answering breath or gasp. I realized then that if he were not breathing on his own, a moonflower would do nothing for him. Neither would the spare breather I still had hanging from my belt.

There was only one thing I could do, and even so I didn't know if I would be too late. But I had to try.

With trembling fingers, I grasped the edges of his hood and flung it back.

Even though I knew time was my enemy, I paused for a second, staring down at him. For he was beautiful.

Alien, yes, from the high, sharp cheekbones to the longish flattened nose. His eyebrows arched, black against black, above crescents of dark lashes. And his skin was dark as night, yet shimmered with iridescence like an oil slick on midnight waters, his face and throat covered in scales so fine I almost didn't realize what they were at first.

All this I took in, and then I lifted the breather from my face and bent down and pressed my mouth against his, breathing the warmth and oxygen from my own lungs into his body, willing him to accept the gift. *Breathe, damn you!* I thought.

Live.

His mouth was slack against mine, unmoving. I gulped more air from the breather and forced it into him once again, locking my lips on his, pushing every ounce of oxygen I could spare into his mouth. And then he began to cough, his lean frame racked with the struggle to get the good air in, and I immediately lifted my head and slapped the spare breather over his mouth and nose.

"What the hell were you thinking?" I demanded, the anger in my voice somewhat diminished by the tinny quality of the speaker in the breathing apparatus. Hot moisture mingled with the stinging rain on my cheeks, and I realized I must have been weeping as I bent over him.

He coughed again and shook his head. I didn't know whether it meant he had no answer for me, or simply that he hadn't recovered enough for speech.

One thing I did know was that I needed to get him inside. Somehow I found my way past all the heavy, water-logged robes to slide an arm around his torso and half pull and half drag him to his feet. He clung to me, the rasping of his breaths magnified by the apparatus covering his nose and mouth.

Each inch seemed like a foot, each yard a torturous mile. One hitching step after another, we made our way back to the airlock at the rear of the house, and from there on into the greenhouse. It was warmer inside, but I didn't know whether the air circulation system had compensated yet for the disastrous loss it had suffered while it was open to the outside. Certainly the plants still drooped, although I supposed it was too soon for them to have begun to revive.

So we pushed on to the main part of the house,

where I limped Sarzhin into his study, as it was the room closest to the greenhouse. Besides the desk and chairs and various small tables scattered about, it had a large electrical fireplace with a sofa placed conveniently in front of it. I deposited him there and then located the remote for the fireplace. It roared into life as soon as I clicked the button, flames dancing in shades of blue and green over a bed of frosted glass.

No doubt the water from Sarzhin's robes would ruin the upholstery, but the couch was the warmest place I could think of. Certainly I didn't have the strength to drag him all the way up the stairs to his rooms.

Almost as soon as he was seated on the sofa, he reached toward the hood of his cloak, as if he meant to pull it back up around his face.

"It's a little late for that, isn't it?" I asked.

He paused then, and slowly lowered his gloved hands to the breather, which he lifted away and set down on the cushion next to him. "I suppose it is." His voice was hoarse, with none of its usual richness.

I found myself wanting to stare at his features, at the way the firelight caught those delicate scales and shimmered with glints of sapphire and emerald. His eyes were blue, a startling cobalt against his black skin.

Instead, I moved a little closer to the hearth and tried to tell myself I wasn't quite as cold as I thought I was. That didn't work too well—I ended up sneezing and sending a fine spray from my wet hair as my head jerked from the violence of the sneeze.

"You're soaked," he said.

"So are you."

"True." He reached up toward his head, to the sodden black mass of his hair. For the first time I realized it was actually quite long; most of it had been caught into a clasp of dark metal at the nape of his neck, but some straggling pieces had escaped and clung wetly to his neck. "You wish to talk. I understand. But I propose we both get ourselves more in order first. In the library in one half-hour?"

My lips parted as I began to voice a protest, and then I stopped myself. He was right—it would be foolish to sit here in our wet clothes and try to sort all this out. As much as I hated to delay, I didn't want either him or me to catch cold. If Zhores even got sick. We Gaians could cure a cold within a day, but so far there still wasn't a workable vaccine.

I nodded. "A half-hour."

Despite having to dry my hair back to something resembling normality and having to strip to my skin and work my way back out with all clean, dry clothes, I was still the first to enter the library.

It appeared Sarzhin had given some orders to the mech, however, since another fire burned in the hearth here, and on a table that sat between two small divans was a square bottle and two fragile-looking glasses that had to be antiques of some kind. I moved closer so I could see the label on the bottle, but the words on it were written in a heavy, flowing script I didn't recognize.

"It is called *zharis*," came Sarzhin's voice, and I looked up to see him enter the room, once again in the familiar black robes. He had left the hood down, though, and met my curious gaze directly.

"From your home world?" I asked.

"Yes." He moved past me and picked up the bottle, then removed the silvery stopper that sealed it. When he poured the liquid from it into the two glasses, I saw the *zharis*, whatever that was, had a pale green hue that seemed quite alien here on Lathvin, where everything was gray and black and dark red.

He handed a glass to me, and I lifted it gingerly to my nose and sniffed. It smelled sweet and delicate, and rather like some of the flowers he raised in his greenhouse.

"It is quite safe, I assure you. It is considered a gift between friends, back on Zhoraan."

After a statement like that, I knew I couldn't do anything except take a sip. So light it felt more that I was inhaling it rather than actually drinking it, the *zharis* slipped over my tongue in a burst of effervescence, and then left a trail of tingling warmth down my throat.

Sarzhin watched me as I drank, and for some reason I felt terribly self-conscious, as if it had been I who had hidden her face all this time and was only now revealed. Those startling blue eyes were grave, intent. A heat that had nothing to do with the *zharis* flooded my cheeks as I glanced from his eyes to his mouth and recalled the touch of his lips against mine. Yes, I'd been trying to save his life, but now—

Now I wanted to lay my mouth against his again, and for an entirely different reason. I hadn't wanted to think it, had tried to couch my feelings in insipid terms such as "fond" or "like," but those horrible moments when I thought I might have lost him had taught me a very different story.

I cradled the delicate glass between my palms, and then said, "Why?"

His mouth lifted slightly at one corner. "Only one 'why'?"

"I thought I'd let you decide which one to answer first."

Sarzhin chuckled a little then; somehow it sounded different when it wasn't muffled by the folds of his hood. "I thought you weren't coming back."

"We missed the shuttle. My stupid sister and her stupid shopping trip—" I broke off and watched him lift his own glass. He still wore the gloves, I noticed. "It certainly wasn't enough for you to kill yourself over!"

"Wasn't it?" He drank a little of the *zharis*, then added, "Perhaps I answered the wrong 'why.' Let me start over."

I nodded. "That might be a good idea."

He smiled. His teeth looked human enough, although I got the impression that there were somehow more of them than in a regular human mouth. "The Zhore are empaths, Anika. Not telepaths—we cannot read minds—but we do sense emotions. Among other Zhore, this is not an issue, as we have had millennia of practice protecting ourselves and refraining from unrestrained projection of emotion. Out in the galaxy at large, however, we are at a disadvantage. This is why you see us go cloaked and hooded as we do; the very weave of our garments contains elements that block some of these emotions. But this is also why we don't allow off-worlders on Zhoraan."

It made some sense, I supposed. But his answers only brought up more questions. "Then why live here at all? I would think your people would feel uncomfortable if they were surrounded by humans." Never mind the little matter of inviting me into his house, or repeatedly asking me if I would be his wife. One would have thought a member of an empathic race would have done everything possible to protect his isolation. Now I was beginning to be very glad I had come here after all, but that didn't explain why he had requested my presence in the first place.

"You'll notice that I have no near neighbors," Sarzhin replied. Then he shook his head. "That is no real answer. The truth is—" He hesitated, and again regarded me carefully. "The truth is that our population has been declining for some time. Our scientists have applied themselves to the problem, as you might well imagine, but as of yet they have found no solution. One thing they did discover, however, is that the Zhore are compatible with humans. Biologically, that is."

For a few seconds my brain didn't quite know how to process that particular piece of information. Then it caught up, and I said, "Oh." Well, I supposed that explained why he kept asking me to marry him. Or did it? After all, marriage wasn't exactly a necessary prelude to procreation.

"'Oh,' exactly." Another smile, but this one looked rather grim. He lifted his glass and took another drink before continuing, "For my people, though, it is one thing to know your race is compatible with another in the purest genetic sense, and quite another to make the mental leap necessary to do anything about it, especially for a people as reclusive as the Zhore. The dispute over Lathvin provided an opportunity, however—we were given a chance to live among you and attempt to see if such unions were at all feasible."

I reflected then that the Zhore had an odd way of going about the process. After all, it's sort of hard to meet people when you're holed up in a mansion all the time. I certainly had yet to see a Zhore hanging out in the Filling Station and offering to buy the women getting off-duty from the commissary or the GRC's office a round of drinks. I refrained from saying so, however, and waited for Sarzhin to continue. After so many months of mystery, it was a relief to finally be getting some answers from him. And after seeing him lying there, still and silent, I wanted to hear his voice, if only to reassure myself that he was all right and hadn't done any irreversible damage to himself.

"I had sensed you," he told me, and his eyes met mine and held. For a second I felt as if I might drown in those depths, blue as the world where I had been born and yet could not remember at all. "Faintly, of course, but still,

I knew when you drove past, felt your comings and goings. This was the first sign, the first realization that compatibility with a human might be more than simply biological. I could not think how to approach you, though. Others of my kind have encountered similar difficulties."

That didn't seem too surprising. After all, if your entire race makes it a habit to keep to themselves, then any outward sign of changing its behavior would of course be met with suspicion. All Sarzhin could do was wait, and hope for a chance—

"You didn't—you didn't make my father have that accident, did you?"

Sarzhin's eyes widened, and he said immediately, "No, of course not. You saw how bad the weather was."

"Yes," I replied, suddenly ashamed I could even have thought that of him. I wanted to step forward, reach out to touch him, but somehow I couldn't quite work up the nerve. Maybe, since he was an empath, he'd be able to pick up from me that I wanted more contact than I'd previously allowed. "I've never seen a storm like that, before or since."

But he made no move toward me. "While I did not cause the accident, I did take advantage of it, and for that I must apologize. By then I'd begun to feel quite desperate, as the months and years went by, and I found no way to initiate a meeting with you."

I wanted to tell him—what, that it was all right? That blackmailing my father was a small thing compared to being a member of a race that was slowly dying and needed to do whatever it could to survive? The ends never justified the means, or so I had been taught, but I understood what he had done even if I couldn't completely condone it.

"Is that why you settled where you did?" I asked. "So that you would be near a homestead with two daughters?"

"That was why I chose the site initially. Lathvin presented a number of difficulties, among them being the sparseness of the settlements here. To have two young women nearby increased the odds, although I did not count on your sister going off-world to attend college. That turned out to be of no import, because it became obvious to me soon enough you were the one who mattered."

As much as I wanted to reach out to him, one logical part of my brain was crunching the numbers and coming up with a sum I didn't like very much. "So I was just supposed to be...what? Convenient breeding stock?"

At once he came to me and took my hands in his gloved ones. "Oh, no, Anika. You misunderstand. While some races may go about such things coldly or carelessly, it is not that way for my people. We must be truly one with our partners, or there can be no consummation, no children. It was only by having you here with me, and learning who you truly are, that I could confirm we were compatible. I felt that we were. My soul told me so, but it also told me to be patient."

That reassured me a little, but something else occurred to me. "Then why ask me to marry you from the beginning? Why not wait and see how things progressed?"

"You'll notice that I did change my course midway, after you requested it." He shook his head—at himself, I was fairly certain. "Eagerness, I suppose. I knew from the second you crossed the threshold that you were the one. I suppose I hoped you would have a similar reaction, even though such things are not as common in humans. I soon learned I was wrong—and yet, the way you responded to me each day told me something more about you. I saw a change in you, a gradual softening, even if you did not yet recognize it yourself. It gave me hope."

I couldn't deny that. The truth had come to me slowly, but even during those months of willful ignorance I had seen a change in my feelings toward him, from alien captor to fond companion. It had only required a crisis to allow me the final realization of what he meant to me.

He gazed down at me, hands still wrapped around mine. "And so you became a part of my life, your spirit so interwoven with mine that when I said it was impossible for you to be away any longer than three days, I told you the truth. With you gone, I would die."

He spoke simply, as if relating a fact so obvious it needed no further explaining. I shivered then, thinking of how close it had been. Damn Libba and her carelessness! It was, I realized then, something I had always overlooked before that moment. My sister thought of herself first—not maliciously, but with an airy disregard for the things other people might consider important. It was what had spurred her to stay on as a graduate student, even though I'd been itching to get off Lathvin, and it was that same heedlessness which had allowed her to dismiss my concerns about getting back on time.

Because of her, Sarzhin had almost died.

Because of her, I had almost lost everything. Only now was I beginning to understand how terrible a loss it would have been. Not just for me, but for his people as well.

"I'm so sorry," I murmured. I blinked then, watching as his dark form began to dissolve in a blur of tears. "So, so sorry."

And then he did pull me toward him at last. Surely he must have known how much I wanted him to hold me. Truly, my need in that moment must have been so obvious that even a non-empath could have sensed it. His arms went around me, and he pulled me close. His touch seemed somehow familiar, no doubt because of the echoes from that one dream, but the reality was far better. Under the robes he wore a close-fitting dark tunic of a softer weave than his outer garments, and I laid my head against his chest and listened to the beating of his heart. It seemed to be located on the opposite side from a human's, but the sound itself was familiar enough. He smelled good, too, of something warm and woodsy that somehow reminded me of the greenhouse and its rows of lovingly tended plants and herbs.

Just the softest brush against the top of my head, a feather touch telling me he had placed his lips there. I tightened my arms around him, and we stood, clinging to one another, for some time. Finally, though, he pulled away—only a little, so he could gaze down into my face. I stared up at him, at every elegant line of his features, at the mouth I wanted so much to taste.

He said, "I've asked you the same question many times before. May I ask it again now?"

I nodded, but told him, "Only kiss me first."

As quick as lightning his lips met mine, and there was something electric in the shock that meeting sent through me. I hadn't realized a kiss could be like this, where every nerve ending in your body seemed to catch fire, and the universe narrowed down to the perfect symmetry of his lips against yours. What would come next, I couldn't begin to guess, but it didn't matter. Nothing mattered, except that I could finally give him the answer he'd been waiting so long to hear, the answer I had been hiding in my heart all that time, even if it had taken far too long for me to recognize the truth of my love for him.

"Oh, yes," I told him, and watched his blue eyes seem to light from within. "Yes, Sarzhin, I will marry you."

And again our mouths touched as his swirling robes surrounded me with their warmth. We kissed for a long moment, until he lifted his lips from mine and pulled me close against him. Within that embrace, I knew I was safe, and loved. I also knew some people would never understand, that they would look on Sarzhin and see him only as an alien, and not the person who had become everything in the world—the universe—to me. Some of them would very likely be my own family members. But I would face those problems when the time came. For now it was enough to feel the lift of Sarzhin's chest beneath my cheek, to know how precious every breath was. I had almost lost him. I would not take that chance again.

"And what now?" I asked. "A big wedding with flowers and overpriced food?"

He smiled down at me. I found myself fascinated by the shimmer of his skin, the way the light caught in the little crinkles at the corners of his eyes when he smiled. All those months, I had never known such beauty hid itself beneath the heavy dark robes.

"My people's ways are not your ways," he replied. "When souls have communion, there is no need for laws and documents and forced celebrations."

"Thank God," I said frankly. "Because after listening to Libba natter on about seating arrangements for the past few days, I'm pretty much done with weddings. I'd love to do it the Zhore way."

"Then come with me."

He took me by the hand and led me out of the study, up the stairs and down the corridor. We passed the doorway to my rooms, headed to the one place in the house where I had never been. His chambers.

Again I had a flash from my dream, of that empty room with the cold wind blowing through it, but I told myself not to be ridiculous, that Sarzhin was right here with me, and everything was fine. Better than fine, really.

Those foolish concerns disappeared as soon as he

opened the door. For instead of the barren spaces I had dreamed, I saw a room filled with green, with living things everywhere. The air was moist and rich, and smelled of delicious off-world flowers.

I blinked, and realized the effect came from vining plants that grew from cunning planters on the wall, as well as more of the wall fountains Sarzhin—or perhaps it was every Zhore—seemed to love. Underneath was a carpet as soft and thick as the greenest grass from Gaia's fabled meadows. I saw a bed hung with airy fabric in the same elusive blue-green color as the coverlet in my own room, and on the far wall a fireplace sheltered another glass-bed hearth, this one also shimmering in shades of aqua and green.

Sarzhin led me to the fireplace. He reached up and undid the clasp at his neck, and the heavy robes dropped to the floor and puddled at his feet. Somehow he seemed even taller without them; now that the hooded cloak was gone, leaving only the close-fitting tunic and pants behind, I could see just how well-built he was, slender and strong.

"I told you how my people wear their robes to protect themselves from the emotions of others," he said. "But we do not hide ourselves from our life partners. I could not reveal myself in this way until now."

I nodded, but waited for him to go on. As much as I wanted to be with him, I couldn't help experiencing a slight shiver of unease. After all, who knew what rituals the Zhore practiced in private?

"Nothing all that exotic," he told me.

My mouth dropped open slightly. "I thought you said the Zhore weren't mind readers."

"We're not. But the combination of your emotions and the look on your face is easy enough to read."

"I guess we're not going to have a lot of secrets."

Another one of those heart-breaking smiles. "No."

He removed his gloves and dropped them on top of the discarded cloak, and then reached out and took my hands in his. It was the first time our fingers had touched in this way, bare skin to bare skin. Now I could feel the heat of his touch much more clearly, sense how smooth and yet sensual all those little scales were, pressed against my own human flesh.

"I give myself to you," he said. A pause, followed by a little glint in those gleaming blue eyes. "Now you."

"I give myself to you," I repeated.

"Wholly."

"Wholly."

"In this life and the next."

So the Zhore had some belief in an afterlife. I scolded myself for making anthropological observations at a time like this and said, "In this life and the next."

"So it is."

"So it is."

This time the touch of his lips on mine was gentler, but the kiss lasted longer, as if to demonstrate how enduring our union would be. And when he raised his head to break the touch, it was not the end, but only the beginning, because he reached down and lifted me as if I weighed nothing, taking me to the fabric-hung bed and laying me down. I reached up to him, and his weight was on me, our mouths coming together again. My dream hadn't told me he would taste so good, nor that I would be just as eager to reach out and undo the clasps of his tunic as he was to loosen the buttons at my neckline and pull the garment over my head.

His skin was beautiful, sending out tiny glints of jewel colors against a background of pure black. I could only hope he'd think as charitably of my pale indoor skin.

"You are beautiful," he murmured. "In every way, my Anika."

"Mind reader," I teased.

And there was no more time for words, only bodies touching, and the empty spaces in my soul finally filled. Afterward, we held each other for a long time. His chest rose and fell beneath my cheek, and I thanked whatever powers in the universe which might exist that I had not lost him, that I had returned in time to save his life.

I realized then that I might have saved him, brought him back from the darkness with the gift of those life-giving breaths…but in entrusting me with his heart, he had saved me as well.

THE END

Other Books by Christine Pope
(in reverse order of publication)

Blood Will Tell
Science fiction romance
A Gaian Consortium Novel
"Nobody writes feisty heroines and sexy alpha males like Christine Pope, and in this planet-hopping blend of science fiction and romance, she brings enough heat to reverse entropy.–Katherine Tomlinson, author of *Toxic Reality* and *L.A. Nocturne*

Heart of Gold
Steampunk romance
"...a splendid, exciting gaslight romantic adventure, with just a hint of steampunk...gloomy castles, daring escapes, and more excitement than you'd find in a penny dreadful. I found it almost impossible to put down."–Joanne Renaud

No Return
Romantic suspense
The classic story of the Phantom of the Opera comes alive once again in this contemporary retelling by romance author Christine Pope."This novel shows that love will (and can) find a way. Everyone deserves to be loved, and to find love, and if you still believe in love...then this book is for you!" (Amazon review)

Bad Vibrations
Romantic/paranormal suspense
"*Bad Vibrations* will remind readers of Janet Evanovich's early Stephanie Plum novels with its breezy tone, delightful characters, and romantic suspense plot"—Katherine Tomlinson, author of *L.A. Nocturne* & *Toxic Reality*

Sympathy for the Devil
Paranormal romance
"…Such a joy to read I would recommend this book to any-one…I spent an entire afternoon reading this gem and would do it again in a heartbeat." — ParaNormalRomance.org

Playing With Fire
Paranormal romance
"This was a fantastic story with an interesting twist: the demons that are the main players are actually quasi-good guys…This is exactly what a novella should be: interesting, enjoyable, plot-filled and short." — Bitten by Books

Fringe Benefits
Contemporary romance
"An interesting story that takes place in fast-paced L.A. and gives the reader a glimpse of the glamorous life. I was intrigued by Pieter…he had a magnetism that draws the reader in." — Single Title Reviews